Outer Core

Sigal Ehrlich

Cover designed by Matthew Phillips (http://thecoverlure.com/)
Cover art:
Copyright © Shutterstock 000022050959

Editing by Nicole Hornbaker Langston
Jenny Sims of www.editing4indies.com

Formatted by Polgarus Studio http://www.polgarusstudio.com/

Published by Sigal Ehrlich
http:// www.sigalehrlich.com

Visit the author website:
http://www.sigalehrlich.com

Version 2016.04.15

For my readers.

Also, for Shachar, my real-life Ian.

Table of Contents

To reach the core of inner beauty,
one must first unravel the many protective layers.

No matter what, relationships will always be haunted by mistakes we've made and wrongs we've hurt each other with. And you can only hope, as the legendary Bob D. sang, that you'll have a strong foundation when the winds of change shift . . . and boy, these winds of change are shifting. Shifting and bringing a big pile of change with them as they swift by change that I can't anticipate. Change I can't protect myself against.

Chapter 1: Prolonging the Inevitable

"What's crappening? What you gorgeous ladies doin'?" Ian's voice booms from my cell.

"Nothing much, just breaking our backs working on our tan lines." I turn to lie on my stomach, facing the sea. "I'm watching Daniel surf. Tash's reading."

"Now, you're talking. Please tell me you're at a nudist beach and describe every piece of stretched skin, smooth skin, foreskin, ridge, rim, and vein you see. . .

"Jeez, I'm so horny, I could do a goat. And that man of yours . . ." Ian adds and sighs. A sigh I could easily constitute as a moan. "Looks like he might be holding some fine stallion in his stable."

Tasha shakes her head, snatching the phone from its resting place on the straw mat we're most indulgingly sprawled across. "No, Ian. Seriously, boundaries! That's her *fiancé* you're talking about!" she squeaks.

Ian laughs it off. "Newsflash, Barbie. The fact he's spoken for doesn't mean he can't be healthily appreciated . . . every part of him, that is. *Every part.*"

"You're too much this early in the morning; speak to Hales."

Tasha scrunches her nose, handing me the phone. "I'm getting back to my book." She slides her sunglasses from her head back to cover her eyes.

"What's she reading?" Ian asks with a chuckle, his voice colored with horn sounds and bustling street bedlam.

"One of those I'm so in love with you I can't breathe, it's you, it's always been you, but your stepbrother is oh-so-hot, so let's have a ménage kind of literary gems."

Ian snorts a laugh while Tasha raises her hand to show me her middle finger, not even bothering to glance my way.

"All the heroines in these books are practically snails, Tash. Snails!" Ian hollers.

A "Huh?" rolls out of our mouths in unison. Tasha pivots her head, her eyes jumping from the device in my hand to my shrug.

"Softies! No spines. Leaving trails of slime in every scene the hero, pardon, *alpha*, breathes their way."

I giggle, my eyes drawn to Daniel catching yet another wave, adeptly riding it with utter grace and heightened sex appeal. His damp, mussed hair highlighted with streaks of gold by the warm sun. All of a sudden, the "trails of moisture" part doesn't sound so ludicrous. Still drinking up the delectable sight that is my fiancé, I ask, "So how's the Big Apple treating you?"

"I'm heading to a meeting with the director as we speak," Ian says, excitement lacing his words. "God, it's like the worst part of Shitville up here. It's so raucous and gray," he murmurs next. "I still can't believe this is really happening. Crazy, eh?"

And we're back to the original subject.

"I'm so happy for you. I was beyond stoked when I saw your ugly face on a billboard, but a movie; that's mind blowing."

"Yeah. I hope everything goes smooth, and there'll actually be a movie." His voice takes a weaker, self-conscious tone.

"Just be yourself."

"Dah. Okay, gotta go. Sharky's here."

"Bye," Tasha and I chorus. "Knock 'em dead."

I smile at Ian's perfect accolade for his agent. Stanton Cohen, aka Sharky, is indeed a personified shark. Smooth. Sharp teeth and tongue, a bona fide swindler who threads the big league's media waters leaving casualties behind. And while he's at it, he clinches the best deals for his clients.

Tasha closes her Kindle and turns to lie on her back, covering her face with an impossibly large, floppy straw hat. "I feel like I need a break," she says to the skies.

I crane my neck and give her a side-glance, finding nothing but a hat made of straw and plump lips. "A break from what, missy?"

"I don't know." She sighs

"Work, home, life?"

"Rafa, I think. And, well, yeah, him."

I turn to mimic her position, lying on my back, and close my eyes to block out the blinding sun. "Why, what happened?"

There's a moment of utter silence, besides the faint echoes of birds' chirping and waves swooshing. "Nothing happened. That's the thing."

"Not sure I'm following."

"Sometimes, it feels like I'm with Ian when I'm with Rafa." The tail end of her sentence comes out on a softer chord.

"What do you mean?"

"I mean we have this great chemistry in every aspect of our relationship, yet it feels more like a sibling sort of connection rather than what it's supposed to be."

"That sounds like a great foundation for a relationship to me."

"No." She sighs again. "Not when there's no tension whatsoever."

"What tension?"

"The tension that controls your excitement. The kind that makes you want to rip his clothes off when you see him. I don't have this thrill bubbling up in me before seeing him. I'm always glad to see him, don't get me wrong. But . . ." She huffs. "There's no anticipation. Zero anticipation. You know what I mean?"

For some meditative beats, I ponder her words and my reaction to Daniel. Tasha's concern crystalizes. Regardless of how long we've been together, even if Daniel is in the next room, I miss him. A constant light with his name on it buzzes within me. "Yeah, I think I get what you're saying. So what are you going to do about it?"

"Dunno. Guess I need a short break. Some time apart. A getaway to think things over. Somewhere I'd be slathered in creams and oils till I die of happiness. Besties are a part of the package, of course."

"I hear ya." I nod though she can't really see me from under The Hat. "Let me talk to Mr. Hollywood and see what we can do. See if his tight schedule can accommodate simple ol' us." She sends her hand to her hat, raises it enough to send me a gigantic grin that ends with a glitzy smile, and then returns to hide under the ridiculous accessory.

"So did Daniel mention anything about setting a date again?" Tasha asks out of the what-in-the-literal-hell blue, making me wince. *What's up with killing the serene quietude, missy?*

"No, but it's probably coming. Actually, I'm surprised he's dropped it for a while now." I bet it's a new tactic of his to keep me numb, sedated with sex and bliss before the next strike.

"Hales, really, what's your problem? Honestly, I don't get you. And please don't give me the whole finding yourself first thing. It might work for Krishna chicks. Otherwise, it's just lame."

Seeing Daniel's handsome face before my closed eyes, I look for some illumination to what's been holding me from finally setting a date for our wedding. I don't even have the slightest of doubts in my mind about marrying him. But still. "I don't know," I say in mild frustration.

"You're so maddening."

"Excuse me, missy? Whose side are you on anyway?"

"*Yours*." By her tone alone, I can just imagine the hole she would have burned into me with her stare if that absurd hat didn't have her buried. "Grow a pair and just do it."

"Grow a pair and do what?" Daniel's voice timbres from somewhere above, prompting me to send my hand to shade my eyes and look up at him. In tandem, Tash resurfaces from under her straw accessory. With one powerful shove, Daniel secures the surfboard in the sand and sends his hand to the zipper at the back of his wetsuit.

He halts with the suit peeled down to his waist when Tasha says, "Told your lady love here that the whole stalling to set a date for the wedding is getting old."

And then there were two. I'm officially disowning her. As of this moment, it's just Ian and me. But first things first. I must comment on this treason before my not so subdued beloved psycho has a field day with it. And since there's no better distraction than seduction, I jump to my feet to jump him. Before he is able to comment or breathe, I stretch up on my tiptoes and glue my lips to his. Drops from his damp hair rain down on me as our kiss gains momentum. Breaking the kiss, I say, "Hey, you'll get me all wet," while adding a sultry hue to my voice.

"You bet your sweet, sweet, perfect ass I will," he whispers in my ear.

Bingo, we are in the sexy innuendoes realm. Mission

accomplished, distraction achieved. I grin at him, licking my lips from the wonderful taste of D mixed with sea.

"I'll leave you ladies to it. I'm going to hit the shower." Daniel kisses me again. He brings his lips to my cheek, kisses it once more, and shifts to nuzzle me just below my ear. "Just so you know, your little attempt at diversion didn't work. We'll talk later." He turns to get his board and walks back to the house.

Damn you, Tash.

. . .

"Hey, check out the text Ian just sent us," Tasha says over a giggle while putting her cup into the dishwasher. As she turns to look for her flip-flops and car keys, I ask her for her phone.

I send Daniel a soft smile when he enters the kitchen, heading to the fridge. Trying not to read too much into the halfhearted smile he rewards me with, I check the message.

"What?" I study the screen. "I can't believe this, this is such . . . *Aaargh!*" I express my feelings to the tabloid link Ian sent us which he captioned with "my day = made."

I narrow my eyes at Tasha, an action that makes her laugh even harder. "C'mon, Hales, it's hilarious."

"No, nothing is even remotely funny about it. It's . . . *ugh!*" I give the photo of Daniel and me a better examination. It is from one of the formal events we attended recently, and we are smiling at each other. He looks spectacular in a tux while I look more than cute in a little black dress. Everything about the photo is lovely. Everything minus one small detail. Somehow, they managed to capture my body in the most uncomplimentary angle. Something about the way I'm standing gives the illusion of a prominent beer belly.

My narrowed eyes dart Daniel's way at his snort as he checks out the photo. "What?" he says with a chuckle. His grin grows. "Told you one burrito was enough."

"Sure that's the angle you're choosing to go with?" I give him a death look, which only prompts his teasing lips to smirk.

He winks at me. "Looks cute on you, though."

"Who eats a burrito before squeezing into a tight dress?" Tasha asks, incredulous.

"My awesome Hayley." Daniel takes a long swig of his bottled water, his joyful eyes on me.

"Well, what can I say, Hales. Mommy belly indeed looks cute on you," Tasha says still grinning like a loon.

"God, what an awful picture." I tilt the phone sideways to have a better look. "My body looks so disproportional." I groan.

"You always look perfect. I'd take you any shape or size." Daniel squeezes my waist, leaving a kiss on my forehead on his way out of the kitchen.

"Yeah." Tasha scrunches her nose. "Easy to say when Hayley looks like she does."

Daniel turns in the doorway to face Tasha, amusement cleared off his features. "Natasha, I can assure you that I'd want Hayley in any size, and it's a matter of fact, I can't wait for her to have a 'mommy belly.'"

I barely catch Tasha's wide smile as I look at Daniel startled. For a stretched beat, I take a step into myself. The impact of Daniel's words outlasting my next breaths. *I can't wait for her to have a mommy belly?* Is he serious? He can't wait? Does he want to start a family . . . right away? For a span of a confusing moment, a vision of Daniel with a child, our child, takes form before my eyes. Sweet, warm pain brims in my chest. I stand still, jarred. Something happens inside of me; something catalyzes deep, deep inside me. Tasha squeezes my hand with a wide grin, her eyes following Daniel as he leaves the room.

"We still need to talk," Daniel says over his shoulder, his tone shaking me out of a tailspin of thoughts.

Chapter 2: Making Amends

After seeing Ms. Traitor-Taylor to her car and starting the dishwasher, I turn to face my fate. I find him in his office ending a call. Leaning on the doorjamb, I watch Daniel. He's too absorbed in the call to notice me. A smile blooms on my face as I gaze at him running a hand through his unruly golden clusters, looking deliciously casual in a white tee and jeans as he gazes out the window. He scrubs his hand over his scruff, not seeming too pleased with the response coming from the speakerphone. With an irritated sigh, he swivels in his chair and turns to brace his elbows on the table, steepling his fingers above the phone.

"I see. Then if there's any problem, this is my number," he says, blatantly impatient.

"Mr. Stark, you called from an unlisted number," mutters the person on the speakerphone.

"Exactly."

Inwardly, I shake my head. *There are some things about you, D, that I might never get used to.* When he turns to look my way, his features shift into question.

"You are so cute," I state, referring to his refined form of communication with . . . basically, everyone on the planet. A hint of a smile plays at the corner of his lips, and the question in his stare sharpens. "Cute as a button!" I add.

He snorts a brief chuckle. His stare on me turns into something I'm unable to decode. It's somewhere between good-sexy heated, and bad-I'm-about-to-snap hot.

Taking slow steps toward him, I softly ask, "Yes?"

He crooks his finger, signaling for me to come closer. When I'm a step away, he sends his hands to my waist to pull me closer still. Effortlessly, he lifts me to perch on his desk before him. He gazes up at me in solemn concentration. I return his gaze with equal intensity. His hands find my thighs, and he jerks me closer to the edge of the mahogany surface. Daniel pushes the fabric of my loose skirt up exposing my thighs. He leans his face in to leave a kiss on both. Slowly, his mouth makes its way up, leaving my skin burning in its wake. Three more kisses and he drops his forehead to rest on my stomach. I thread my fingers through his hair, waiting. Daniel inches to sit straight, stern hazel eyes unblinking for a few moments.

I clear my throat. "So what's the sentence for my misdemeanor?"

"Hayley . . ." His mouth remains slightly agape as though calibrating a response, and he snaps it shut.

"Daniel?" His name on my lips is a cautious question. A soft and concerned question.

"Forget it. It's nothing." He takes a generous breath.

Oh, how I wish he'd confront me. I even prefer him snapping at me than this reaction. This loaded silence. I shake my head. "No."

His eyes narrow at me, and his jaw clutches.

"Talk to me."

"What about?"

"Daniel . . ."

"What do you want me to say, Hales? I've said everything I had to say. Clearly, I cannot do anything more if you simply chose not to listen."

Ouch. The wedding. Setting a date has been, and apparently still is, a moot subject.

"Well." Daniel rises to stand. He holds his hand for me and helps me jump off the table. "I need to get some work done for tomorrow."

"I love you," I say before leaving, still harboring the leaden feeling in my belly.

"Love you too, Hales," he says with a sigh, giving me a look that makes my stomach twinge once again.

Chapter 3: Grand Gesture

I'm used to waking up alone in the middle of the night. What with Daniel's nocturnal tendencies to burn the midnight oil. He claims he's a night person and most productive in the wee hours of the night. I can vouch for that. He's definitely exceedingly productive at night. You'd never hear me complain. But somehow, with how we left things this time, his absence in our bed niggles me. I call for him, but no answer comes in return. Shrugging on one of his tees, I make my way to the office then to the gym.

"Daniel?" I call out as I take a few groggy steps into the kitchen. I hug myself and move on to the living room. A soft, chilly breeze coming from the open balcony door brushes against my skin, making my stare wander toward the patio. Toward where Daniel lounges on one of the recliners, focused on the notebook on his thighs. "Hey," I say in a supple voice, nearing him. "I missed you in bed," I add, studying his serious expression under the screen's glow. Daniel sets the notebook to the wooden floor. Turning to me, he holds out his hand. I take it and plant my knee next to his hip, slowly lowering to straddle his thighs.

"Couldn't sleep?" His tone is low and caressing. His hand comes up to my neck, brushing my hair over my shoulder.

"Yes." I bob my head and bring my hand to his face. "Easier when you're next to me." With the pads of two fingers, I gently trace over the fresh scar sitting high on his right cheekbone. The one he got just a couple of months ago on that notorious trip to Thailand. The one I can't think about without the horrific feeling it brings along.

"Does it still hurt?" I ask. Really meaning *does it still haunt you?*

He shakes his head from side to side, his eyes hovering over my face.

"Do you want to talk about it?"

He shakes his head again and covers my hand with his. He brings our joined hands to rest on his chest. I lean in closer and press a feathery kiss on the scar. Though the event in which he got said mark of injury is nothing but terrifying, I can't get over how sexy it is. Daniel's scars are the most attractive marks I've ever seen, and in equal part so are his non-physical ones. His well-ingrained emotional scars; these imperfections that just make him all the more perfect to me. Daniel's hand trails to cradle my rear, pulling me closer against him. He leans back on the recliner and looks up at me for a silent beat. Slowly, he inches forward, slowly till his mouth finds mine.

My eyes flicker to his as we ease back. "Why won't you talk about it?" I ask in a dainty voice.

"There's nothing to talk about. What happened, happened, and now, it's history." And in his very unique Daniel way of "pouring his heart out," he kisses me again. This time with greater vigor.

When we pull back to catch our breath, I say, "About earlier, what Tasha said . . ."

"Hales." It's a frustrated warning.

"Okay, let's talk about it." Determination lines my voice. It's time we ironed out this impasse of ours. The "setting a date" plight. We can have an attempt at reason. Though it has proven to crash and burn before takeoff each and every time in the past, there's always hope. Heck, if Scientology is a legit religion, most likely the sky is indeed the limit. And before I'm about to state my case, Daniel's gaze turns hard. Yet brimming with something that twists my insides.

"When you get engaged and enter the most significant relationship of your life, it comes with an impending debt to your partner," he says in his husky voice. "A promise you make to each other that you'll eventually have to live up to by committing to the 'till death do you part' phase of your life. By fulfilling your partner's expectations, you grant them a growing old together pledge. For worse or for better. Just like I promise you that I'll always be there for you, have your best interest at heart, do everything in my power to keep you safe, worriless, and mostly, happy, Hales, I do expect you to do the same for me. And this sort of promise essentially gets its official stamp in a goddamn ceremony with a priest."

Counterargument by my side? The defense has no plausible counterargument. No, your honor, the defense is sort of dumbstruck. "It's so important to you," I state rather than question.

He nods. His eyes blaze into mine a grave hazel.

I worry my lips. "It's just something about the ceremony. I don't know. I don't like what people tend to make of it. Somehow, it always turns into a circus. When all it's really supposed to be about is two people certifying their . . . relationship. Their love. Daniel, I'm not trying to . . . ." I huff.

Creases pile up between his brows. "Hales, it was never about the ceremony. Besides finally wearing your engagement ring, nothing on your part has proved to me just how serious you were, are."

I gape at him. His words jarring me. *How can you even imply that, D? You are and you've always been my everything.*

"Give me something. Prove me wrong, Hales. Show me that you feel the same way. That we're heading in the same direction."

A tumultuous whirlwind of contradicting emotions joins forces inside my chest, twisting in my belly, causing my heartbeat to accelerate. I'm confused, affected, and somewhat riled that he doesn't know just how much he means to me by now.

I rise up to my feet. "Fine." It's an irritated breath. "You want me to show you just how much you mean to me. How I see our future together?" I shake my head. "Fine!" I stride toward the house. I storm through the quiet landing till I reach the bedroom's en suite. Yanking open the cabinet above the sink, I rummage through the contents till I find what I'm looking for. My journey back to the deck is no less spiked. "Here." I toss the little package in my hand into the pool.

Daniel's face is a display of utter dismay as he watches my not so well balanced act. It's night. The skies are dark. Dark but clear enough to illuminate the aluminum pack now lamely swimming in the water. I watch Daniel as he scratches his lip with his thumb. His eyes hone in on the little container floating amid little circles formed in the clammy water. He brings his attention back to me, head tilted to the side, one scarred brow arched in question.

"My pills," I say. "You wanted me to show you just how much you mean to me and where we're heading?" My hand falls to my waist, the other gesturing at the pool. "Birth control pills," I add just to make sure my message is clear.

His lips pull up into a grin as he waits for me to go on.

"This is where I see us heading. I want the same thing I wanted before. *You*. You as my fiancé, you as my husband, you as the father of my children." That grin of his turns into a full-on Daniel Stark smile. Crooked, mirthful, brimming sin.

"So?" he asks.

Pardon? My eyes widen. "So?" My head slightly jerks back in bewilderment. "Wasn't this graphic enough for you."

"Oh, it was." He tries to calm his smile with not much success. In a small gesture, he motions with his hand toward the pool. "What does it really mean, though, Hales? Is it effective . . . immediately?" His eyes dance with joy.

"As of tomorrow morning when I need to take one, I guess." I can't keep my lips from stretching wildly in response to his expression.

Daniel rises to stand, and in three confident steps, he is by my side. He grabs me by my hips and lifts me to straddle him. His lips grinning against mine. Over a smile, he presses a kiss to my no less grinning ones. "So no wedding? You're just gonna be my baby momma?"

"Yes to the wedding, just not necessarily in the near future. And certainly positive on the baby momma part."

Daniel chuckles and brings his mouth to cover mine. And then there's just our mouths, hands, the warmth we're transferring into each other, and little needy, breathy sounds of want. When we pull back, Daniel dips his head, leveling our stare. "Are we really doing this?" It's a quiet question, yet carries so much.

My answer comes out even suppler. "Yes."

The tender warmness of his hands frames my cheeks. His voice lightly vibrates between us. "Christ, I love you." His warm, manly scent. The heat of his breath tunneling to my mouth. Some moments are small but hold such great significance.

In response, I tilt my head to feast on his delectable taste. I can feel a smile crawl up Daniel's lips as our lazy kiss subsides.

"What?" I smile at him. I give his mouth a chaste brush.

His lips pull up higher on the side. "Who's gonna clean the pool now that you've littered it?"

I roll my eyes. His smile becomes radiant. And before I know it, he pushes us both into the pool. I yelp at the chilled bite of the water. The "litter" is our last concern as we start peeling clothes off each other in a lustful, hurried pace.

Chapter 4: Good for Your Soul

"There are so many things out there better than monogamy," Ian says to the strawberry daiquiri in his hand.

"Such as?" Tasha asks, leaning back onto the sunbed by the indoor pool, round cucumber slices covering her eyes.

"Um . . . happiness?"

"What's wrong now?" I say, gazing at Ian with mild frustration.

"Oh, those dear, dear days. The good ol' days are gone." Ian sighs a tad too theatrical.

"What's up with the drama? Which old days?" Tasha says drily.

"The 'I saw, I conquered, I came.' *Hard*, days. I feel old."

"So much therapy in that," I murmur.

"Best time to feel this way, uh, Ian? How does Josh feel about you mourning your good old days of debauchery? Bet he's stoked," Tasha says, blunt disapproval coloring her words.

"Fucked-up timing." Ian shakes his head. "Just when I'm surrounded by all these yummy, free-spirited entertainment world individuals. I swear I must have been conceived on a full moon. It's the only explanation for my rotten luck."

"You know what? Even just talking about it is disrespectful to your boyfriend." It's my turn to scold.

"Whateves . . ." Typical Ian dismissal. "So, Tash, dish out. Why have we gathered here today in this fine pampering establishment?"

Now that the most indulging massages have mellowed the three of us to our bones, we can finally attempt to remedy Tasha's *current* "mid-life" crisis sprawled in this scenic spa resort.

In succession, Tasha peels the cucumber circles from her eyes. She straightens in her seat and turns to us. "I felt like taking a breather from, um, everything."

Ian sends me a sidelong glance. I shrug in return.

"For starters, work has taken over my life lately. But the funny part is, I couldn't be more relieved being so tied up with work. I don't have to come up with excuses not to see Rafa."

Ian's brows furrow. "Didn't see that one coming."

"I think we've reached the 'too comfortable with each other' phase too soon. Feels like we're living together and we've been seeing each other for only a few months. The new and exciting stage no longer exists. To me, it feels like I'm with you." Tasha jerks her chin Ian's way. "I feel too comfortable with him. Which in a way is a bit of a turn-off."

I contemplate Tasha's words, not sure she'd be pleased with my finding. And just as I'm about to speak up, Ian beats me to it.

"Honestly, gorgeous, sounds like you're looking for excuses. I've seen you guys together. You can't take your hands off each other. It's been a while since I saw you so into someone. Too good scares you?"

Hey pot, you're sorta calling the kettle black.

Tasha opens her mouth to respond but closes it right back when I add the clincher to Ian's dogma.

"Tash, you said it yourself, you had a lot on your mind lately. No wonder you weren't fully into your relationship. Yet in the middle of all your stress and crazy, Rafa was there for you. As I see it, you're judging whatever it is you're feeling from the wrong angle."

Tasha pouts first, wrinkles her nose, and only then seems to consider what we've just told her. She shrugs. "I don't know. You guys might be right. Maybe." Ian and I trade pleased glances. "Anywho, glad we're here. I really needed this break. The distance."

For some long, silent moments, we each wander off to our own thoughts.

"So." I break the silence. "Could be that the next time we hang out, I might be carrying a little human inside me." Both my friends dart their gaze my way and freeze. Their stunned expressions are almost comical. As if they'd masterfully synchronized their unified shock.

After what seems like the longest stupefied mini-coma, their words crash. The collision sounds like something along the line of, "Wha-yley-Grace-uh? *Hayley*!"

I can't help but classily snort. In a blink, Ian is sitting, squeezed next to my right thigh, and Tasha almost identically scoots closer to my left.

"What in the literal fuck, Hales?" Ian finally manages to utter a coherent question. Language choice aside.

When I finish recounting the night of my theatrical grand gesture tale, Tweedledum and Tweedledee are on the verge of hysterics.

"No. You didn't just throw the pills into the pool. Gorgeous, you're killing me." Ian chuckles viciously.

"You're such a moron." Tasha cracks up yet again. As her

laughter finally winds down, she says, "Wow, that's huge, Hales. So what are you guys, like, trying now?"

In general, I'm not too keen on discussing the intimate parts of my relationship. Though I used to be the "kiss and tell thy besties" kind of gal, with Daniel it's always been different. Everything that happens between us, everything about him, feels deeper, special. Something I prefer to keep between the two of us.

"We need to wait two weeks before, um, trying. I'm not going to get into the details, something about getting off the pill."

"Don't you prefer to tie the knot first?" Tasha asks. "Oh, wow. Your dad is going to flip."

Ian tsks twice, shaking his head from side to side. "A child born out of wedlock; oh sugar, flipping is putting it wildly mildly."

"I don't really mind. The wedding part will happen eventually. And about my dad?" I sigh. "He'll cope."

"What about Daniel?" It's Ian's turn to probe.

"Once he understood just how committed I am to our relationship, he sort of dropped it."

Tasha's brows hide under her bangs. "Really?"

I nod. Wanting to change the subject, I say, "I want to get him something for his birthday. Something special."

"What, like, more special than, say, a human?" Ian asks, making Tasha laugh.

I roll my eyes, though with a hint of a smile. "No, like an actual gift wrapped up with a bow. Something meaningful."

"Isn't his birthday only in a few good months?" Tasha says.

I nod.

"How about an autographed guitar?" she suggests.

I smile pensively. "Not bad."

"Or a car racing thingy," she adds.

"Oh, I got it." Ian straightens up so he can eye us both. "This is gold." He grins excitedly. "Why don't you get one of those hymen reconstructions? Men dig this shit. It's this alpha thing . . ." He lowers his voice to sound more macho, which by itself, even before hearing the rest of his idea, is pretty moronic. "Claim you, puncture your innocence away." He pops the p in puncture.

"How do you even come up with these things?" My tone is placid and even, just as one would speak to a child.

Ian points at his temple and taps twice with the pad of his finger. "A wealth of brilliance."

Tasha, appearing a tad dazed, says, "Just when I think you've reached your crazy quota, you prove me wrong."

And just like that, the perfect idea pops into my mind. The perfect idea for a gift.

Chapter 5: Waiting Game

It's really fascinating how your perception of time varies depending on what lies at the end of the waiting tunnel. These past two weeks have given me enough time to stew over taking this huge plunge into parenthood, and it has slowed time to an achingly volatile pace full of anxiety, questions, concerns, and an undeniable thrill. Most of all, it's made me really, truly think about marriage. About how it's much greater than two people, especially when a child is involved. Unfortunate as it might be, "untying the knot" is not a difficult thing to do these days. A short bureaucratic process and the "till death do us part" becomes a sad poetic memory. However, a child is a completely different sonnet. It's about tying lives together for eternity.

I don't have even a single doubt in my mind that Daniel is the one I want as the father of my future progenies. But cut a girl some slack; this is one humongous commitment. Am I even mother material? Am I ready to screw up another person's life? Thank God for Daniel's heavy loot bag; at least, financing therapy for our dependents won't be an issue.

I give the bright morning and the calm sea one last appreciative glance, polishing off the last spoonful of my fruit salad. The view from our patio will never get old. I carry my plate and Daniel's empty mug to the kitchen and go search for my man.

Wrapping my hands around Daniel's waist, I give his back a small peck. Quickly, my hands find their way to his belt.

"I really need to get going, Hales. I have a flight to catch," Daniel says, throwing another shirt into his carry-on.

Reluctantly, I take a step back. "Well, I have a mouth that's quick . . ." I grin, sensual teasing full on.

"Fuck . . ." is his curt murmur.

"When you put it that way . . . Fuck, it is! You. While I'm on my knees . . ." I smack my lips together and regard him with a small, flirtatious smile.

Shirt frozen in hand, he gazes at me for a silent moment.

I blink with a dash of sass. "Lost your words? Need a moment, D?"

"Yeah, I need a moment, and I'll take it while you pack. You're coming with me."

"Needy, are we?"

"I'll give you needy."

I squeak, finding my blood rushing toward my brain as Daniel swings me over his shoulder. He sets me back to stand on my feet near our walk-in closet.

"Start packing, you don't need much. Shoes, a thong, and drop in a dress or whatever you need in case I decide to take you to dinner before bed."

I wrap my hands around me. "As much as you going all caveman-macho on me gets me worked up, no can do, handsome."

Daniel folds his arms over his chest. "Why's that?"

"I have an important meeting tomorrow morning." I counter his annoyed stare with a determined, hard one. I gaze at him as he fetches his phone and starts scrolling through his contacts. "What are you doing?"

He gives me a brief, stern glance as he says to the phone, "Hey." He chuckles next. "Is your friend with you?" Daniel rolls his eyes. "I don't have the entire day to swap recipes with you. Is he or is he not?" There's a long pause in which Daniel twists his mouth, not exactly the happiest camper. "Then tell him Hayley will not be at work tomorrow."

Excuse me? He *did not* just call my boss's boyfriend. A flash of irritation hastens up my spine.

"Thanks." He ends the call, and with an utter graveness only he can pull, he tells me, "Start packing. We have seven minutes."

With eyes wider than humanly possible, I snap at him. "Seriously, did you just do that?"

"Six and a half minutes. Hales, pack."

I huff in irritation. "Not happening."

Daniel shakes his head.

With his determined psycho face on, he turns to the closet. Grabbing a small carry-on, he shoves a dress of mine inside, some other clothes fly in next. "You want me to get your creams and shit, or are you getting them?" I watch him, stunned, with a well-developing exasperation. He rolls his eyes again, enters the bathroom, and comes out with a bunch of my stuff crammed into his arms and huddled against his chest. Toiletries are dumped unceremoniously into the suitcase. "Do I need to haul your ass over my shoulder again or you coming?"

I wonder how much prison time you get for strangling someone? Not sure how cute I'd look in ginger scrubs. Maybe I'll get Tash and Ian to help hide the body then I won't have to worry if orange is my color.

"Baby, you started this. Own up to your actions."

"Where are *you* going anyway?" I ask.

"*We are going.* DC. Overnight."

Chapter 6: For Real

There's so much to be said about leisure. The most glaringly alarming thing is how addictive it can be. And oh, it can. In the best, mind-numbing ways possible. While Daniel has been busy doing his business thing, I've let myself indulge a couple of hours more in our ridiculously gigantic and pampering suite. The spoiling theme continued throughout the late morning with a heavenly massage, this treatment and that, till it felt borderline immoral. At that breaking point, I dropped everything excessive gratification and took a lovely jaunt into the city. One that began with a double shot, extra hot, thin layer of froth Grande cappuccino and ended with a few good hours at the National Gallery of Art.

I smile at the graying concierge with the penguin tail tux entering the elegant, checker-floored lobby of the hotel. The sweet scent of the humongous orchid arrangements tickles my nose as I pass the threshold of the hotel's lounge where I'm headed to meet Daniel for an early dinner. My brows furrow and an alarm beeps in my head when I spot him. Daniel is sitting at one of the low tables, bent forward, elbows on his knees, absorbed in his cell. Albeit, next to him there's a pretty lady in a red suit who seems ready to accost what's for all intents and purposes known as *mine*. She leans in, in a that's-the-best-view-to-my-cleavage maneuver. She seems to whisper something, nearing her lips to his ear. Daniel frowns, tilting his head sideways to look at her.

I take a few hasty steps to reach them. "Oh hi, are you two in the middle of something? Can I bother for a sec?" My voice dripping with honey.

Daniel raises inquisitive eyes my way, and the lady who I'm about to offer a little hanky to for her drooling condition twists her mouth. She shakes her head, appearing not the least bit delighted with the interruption.

"Sir, excuse me, but would you be so kind as to accompany me to my room?"

The tip of Daniel's mouth slants into a lopsided grin as he slowly rises to stand. I hold my hand out for him. With Daniel's hand in mine, I bend down to near the baffled lady's ear and whisper, "He seems quite potent, no?" I wink at her and turn to give Daniel a quick, sass-coated once-over.

"What did you tell her?" Daniel asks as we exit the ample room.

I smirk, looking at him from under my lashes, the tip of my tongue held between my teeth.

"Hales?"

"That you look like a decent lay."

Daniel shakes his head, his eyes crinkled at the sides. "So, Miss, now that you have me, what would I have to do in your room?" he teases and adds, "Weren't we supposed to have dinner? I'm starving, baby."

"Follow me." I wink at him, exiting the elevator. Swiping the card at the door, I wait for the little green light to come on and push open the door. "The correct question, Sir, is what you wouldn't have to do."

Daniel lets out an animated snort. "Dinner, Hales?" he asks following me into the suite.

"Tada!" I gesture with my hand to the little shindig of a picnic set on the coffee table in the great room.

Daniel takes it in and walks to the table. He leans down to reach one of the domes with two fingers and opens it. "God, I love you," he murmurs to the display of nicely browned, roasted ribs that enrich the room with the most mouthwatering smoky aroma. "So I guess it's staying in tonight." He steals a fry and brings it to his mouth.

"Well, it's actually having dinner with a *Kill Bill* marathon."

"You're fucking perfect." Husky and happy.

"You're not bad either." Flirty and joyful.

We're halfway through the first movie when I leave my snuggly den under Daniel's arm for a quick pit stop.

"Pause it?" Daniel asks from his resting place on the thick carpet, his back leaning against the sofa.

"Nah." I send him a tiny smile. Daniel's warm stare follows me as I bend to take the leftovers of our dinner and set them outside the door. He watches until I disappear in the vast hall en route to the en suite.

When I come back to the living area, Daniel pauses the movie on the screen. His gaze as he leisurely drinks me in causes warmness to spread over my skin. Said stare grows absorbed, even hypnotized, as if the sheer breaths I take put him in a transfixed state.

"Come here." He offers me his hand, his voice a smoky, coaxing command. I slowly bend down to straddle him. We trade silent gazes as I settle myself on his pelvis. His features soften. I tip my head down, locking our stares. An easy smile touches his lips. His hand moves up to thread into my hair, pausing on the nape of my neck. The distracting chime of Daniel's phone breaks our promising moment. His forehead creases as he checks the screen.

"It's okay, get it," I say in a tranquil voice.

Daniel brings the disturbing device closer to his ear. He huffs, pulling me near to nestle on his chest. I inhale the mix of the clean linen and his warm manly scent. His fingers comb through my hair, caressing in little indulging circles as he listens to the person on the other end. Daniel drops his lips to press on the center of my head.

In the warmness of his embrace, my mind drifts back to the subject that has been occupying my every waking hour for the past two weeks. I feel restless and queasy, but in a good way, with what I'm about to share with him.

"Fine." Daniel heaves a bothered sigh. "I'll do the interview. No personal questions, though, Karen. Nothing but the recent announcement. Any deviation from the subject and I'll cut it short." Daniel listens for a few silent moments. "Yes, I fully intend on following that." After another brief exchange, he concludes the call.

"Hey," he says, his mouth grazing my hair.

I take another lungful of his comforting scent and slightly lean back to return his gaze.

"Hey." My voice comes out mildly croaky, hinting at the mini anxiety I'm harboring. "What was that all about? You're giving interviews again?"

His hand slides to the small of my back, falling lower to palm me. "Just this one. I'm looking to pursue this new venture and the media shining some light on it won't be a bad thing."

"What is it?"

"Just some startups we're considering investing in," Daniel says drily, his lips meeting the skin above my collarbone, his hold on me becoming more eager.

I ease back, bringing my finger to his lips. His eyes search mine. A supple smile eases onto my lips. I gaze at him for another lengthened moment. The special glee in his eyes, my glee. The three scars decorating his sharp features. The deepest one on his upper lip, the nearly hidden one on his brow, and the new one high on his tanned cheekbone. Hazel eyes become soulful, drowning into mine.

My voice comes out quiet and throaty. "Two weeks have passed. It's the real deal now."

Daniel cocks his head, eyes still absorbed in mine.

"The next time we . . . get busy."

A low chuckle rumbles between us. "Get busy, Hales?"

"The next time we 'work on a project,' if you will." Daniel chuckles. I smile in response. "It's been two weeks. We're now officially what they call 'trying.'"

When understanding dawns on him, his hands move to cup my face from either side. His silent air speaks louder than any words could. And it makes my heart ache in the most vicious, sweetest of ways. Daniel slowly brings his mouth to hover next to mine.

"Hales." One word, and the multitude of emotions and promises it carries. When our mouths meet, there's something new about our connection. It's deeper, it's powerful, saturated with a profusion of emotions. Everything around us slowly fades away and it's only us.

Daniel and me.

His hands hold my face, his eyes on mine. They travel to my mouth and back again. He slightly cocks his head, ever so gently advancing. I slowly lean forward. A sliver of air separating our mouths, our breath mixing, our stares transfixed. He tilts his head an inch closer, his eyes slowly closing while his mouth softly covers mine. I part my lips, letting him in. The kiss grows deeper and harder. With an urging need to feel him, I slide my hand under his tee, touching his warm skin. But it's not enough. I tug on the fabric, pulling it up. Daniel breaks our kiss to help me discard his shirt. When our stares re-meet, wordlessly we speak of the magnitude of the moment. And the gears shift. As though possessed, with hurried, clumsy hands, we rip each other's clothes off.

On our knees, our bodies bare, facing each other, is when the atmosphere around us shifts. Gently, Daniel lays me back on the carpet. With a reverential hazel stare, he lies above me, his mass held by his stretched arms. Unhurriedly, he leans down to rest on his forearms, his lips just mere inches from mine. As our bodies slowly meet, words are meaningless. Words are not enough to express this overpowering thing that's happening between us. It's our stares, mouths, skin on skin, that give voice to our emotions. We move together, embraced as proximate as our bodies allow. Every stroke, every thrust, every moan, closer, deeper, overwhelming.

Lost in his adoring stare, in the heavenly pleasure he gives me, in the immense, almost impossible to contain love I feel for him and the thought of the potential outcome of our lovemaking, I feel my throat swell. A shiny screen suffuses my eyes when my hands haste to grab his face and pull his mouth to mine.

Deep inside of me, Daniel stills, gazing at me. A creases forms between his eyebrows as he leans in for his lips to kiss the moist trail under my eye. "Hales, I love you so much, it aches. I never want this pain to go away. Nothing feels this incredible."

I swallow hard because it is painfully incredible, and it's a feeling that's scarce and precious beyond comprehension.

"Hales?" Daniel's husky voice pulls me out of my post-ecstasy soaring, blissfully sprawled on his warm body. Lazily, I raise my head from his chest.

"You're quiet . . ."

"Just thinking, you know."

"I hope it will look like you. A mini version of you," he says next.

A smile, the naughty kind, crawls up my lips. "God forbid it will take after its daddy. We'll have a psycho kid."

"I'm giving you a second and a half to take that back. I can't be held accountable for my actions if you don't."

I narrow my eyes at his humored hazel ones. His scarred lip tips up. Before I know it, I'm on my back with an amused Daniel straddling me, holding my hands stretched above my head. I roll my eyes in utter joy. He shifts to hold my hands with one hand while the other travels right to my most ticklish spot.

"No!" I beg through choked laughter, which of course just encourages him to take even greater pleasure in my misery. "Please, Daniel . . ." Nothing. "I take it back," I exhale, trying to even my breathing.

Daniel stops his assault, his lips in a gigantic grin. He dips to press a light kiss on my panting lips. "I never want to do life without you again," he says, shooting a warm surge right through me.

Saying things like that could be irreparable to a girl's heart, D.

Chapter 7: The One Thing

Daniel

It's the third time I've tried to read this damn long email. My thoughts wander with each attempt. Wander off to the one place that sets my mind at ease. A smile tugs at my lips as snippets from last weekend run through my mind. I shake my head grinning. *Fucking surreal*. Hales might be pregnant with my child.

"Mr. Stark, I'm sorry. Can I interrupt for a moment?"

I give Anne a sharp gaze. "It's the kind of question that should be asked at the door, not halfway through the room."

Anne's round cheeks tint with a smear of a pink hue. I sigh and fold my shirt's sleeves to my elbows, waiting for her to speak.

"Do you still want to talk to Ms. Taylor, or would you like me to reschedule the meeting?"

My jaw clutches. "It's on the calendar, right?" I ask, irritation rapidly taking over my patience.

"Um, yes." Her edginess grows. She presses the stack of papers she's holding closer to her chest.

"Why would I want to reschedule then?"

"Okay, I see. I will call her right in." Hastily spinning around, she almost loses her balance and leaves the room. My eyes meet the ceiling.

Waiting for Natasha to come in, I give Hayley's framed photo a quick glance. I can't even try to fight the grin that's spreading on my lips.

Nodding, I gesture for Natasha to take a seat as she greets me.

"Okay, I'll cut to the chase," I say, leaning back in my chair and steepling my fingers.

"Oh, wow . . ." Natasha gapes at me for an absorbing moment, her mouth rounded with surprise. I wait for her to digest everything I just told her, offered her. "Um." She straightens up and wets her lips. "Do you need an immediate answer?"

I shake my head. "I wouldn't expect you to have an answer right away. Think about it. Let's talk again . . . in a week?"

"Yes. A week sounds good." She brushes the non-existent lint from her skirt. "Thanks for thinking of me." She shifts again in her chair. "It's a lot to think about. Wow, I'm honored."

I nod.

She shifts again. "Dani . . . Mr. Stark. Um . . ." She clears her throat. "Sorry. This might come across, um, unprofessional to bring up your personal life," Natasha says hesitantly, squirming in her chair again, appearing not the least bit comfortable.

I nod, telling her I'm listening. The muscle above my jaw working under my skin.

"Does Hayley know? Did you tell her about . . . this?"

I purse my lips. "There's nothing to tell her before you make your decision is there?"

"Right. Right." She breathes, pensive.

I dismiss her. "That will be all."

She gives me another introspective gaze, thanks me again, and leaves the room.

What would Hales say if Natasha decides to . . .

The vibration of my cell on the desk pulls me back from my momentary lapse. Creases pile up on my forehead as I notice the name on the display. *She* never calls me at work . . .

"Everything okay?" I ask in lieu of a greeting. She takes a deep breath. Something about her sigh doesn't sit well with me. "Are you okay?" I repeat, concerned.

As she starts to talk with an undercurrent of a shudder to her voice, my chest tightens.

"I'm coming over," I say after she lays it all out for me. My heart beating at a borderline painful rate.

"No. Not now. I'll call you once I have further details, and we'll see."

I curse under my breath. "I can't be here thinking God knows what, when you're there, alone. I'm coming over."

"Please don't, Daniel. You have your business to run and your . . . Let's wait, okay?" she says, a plea in her voice. "I have to go now." She ends the call.

I throw the phone on the desk and take a breath that doesn't reach all the way through.

Goddamnit. Everything inside me darkens and withers, everything promising and joyful vanishes. I feel like smashing everything in my path. I grab the Veyron's keys and shove them in my pocket. I need to clear my head, and the sooner I get it done, the better. I can't do it here. I don't even tell Anne I'm leaving. I rush out to the only place I know I'll be able to take *this* out.

I text Anne later, before I put on my gloves and confront the inanimate punching bag, asking her to cancel my meetings for the next couple of hours.

I squeeze my eyes tight. Opening them, I give the suspended bag a hostile gaze and start pummeling as though possessed.

Channeling my frustration through my frenetic blows. Sweat covers my temples and upper lip. I swipe my face with the back of the glove and continue taking out my frustration with forceful, fiery precision. As the bag bounces back my way, I grab it with both arms. Hugging it, I rest my forehead on the cold leather. The one thing I feared the most, the one thing that's always been at the back of my mind, lurking in my darkest thoughts, might become a new reality. A reality I'll never be ready to confront.

Chapter 8: That Thing You Do

"Stop it. Shut up already, I'm dying here!" Tasha raises a hand Ian's way, her face flushed from excessive laughter. Looks like Missy's about to pop out a lung.

I shake my head fondly, enjoying Ian's bright grin. He is slouched on our living room sofa, sporting a new bedroom hairstyle, jeans ripped at the knees, and a black t-shirt with "#HIGHANDMIGHTY" plastered on the front. Ian fashion, he resumes his ridiculously hilarious tales of his last visit to the studio responsible for *Urban Heartbreak's* production. Ian's first feature film, something that still blows us away each time we mention it.

Tasha straightens in her seat, hugging one of the throw pillows to her chiffon blouse clad chest. A giggle leaves her mouth to Ian's impersonation of the head of the studio who's apparently a six foot bulky macho with a voice of a fairy princess overdosed on helium. Ian's words, not mine.

Ian brings his hand to his chest. "His shirt was so damn ugly. I felt for it. I really felt for it." He stretches out a hand and pats the air. "It made me want to pat it and tell it everything would be okay," he adds, sending Tasha into another wave of cackles.

My smile gradually fades as I turn to look out the garden doors. My eyes focus in on the glistening pool's water while my mind takes a walk down disquiet lane. The subject of my concern is my significant other who's been a perplexing bundle of contradictions the past week or so. Daniel's behavior has been even less predictable than his usual Jekyll and Hyde delightful self. He's been disappearing too often inside his own head, while other times, he's been too overprotective of me. To a disconcerting degree. Treating me as if I were too fragile to handle . . . life. *What's come over you, D?*

Just as I'm about to rise to stand and check on Daniel, who's been burrowed in his office for the last couple of hours, I'm stopped by Tasha's high-pitched voice. "Hold up, you snorted bleach?" Her eyes wide, darting at Ian.

Ian shrugs in utter nonchalance.

I frown. "What are you talking about?"

"What's wrong with you?" Tasha's nostrils flare.

"Hey, gorgeous, let's pump the brakes a little. Whatever happened to do whatever makes your oil well blow out?" Ian counters.

"What does that even mean?" I murmur. *Oh* . . . I purse my lips at the realization.

"Ian, this is not okay. It's beyond that. First, you talk about all the hot guys at these parties, and now, you're telling me you tried hardcore drugs?" Tasha winces in disapproval. "What in the hell is wrong with you? Seriously, Ian, time to put your thinking cap back on before it's too late."

"Ian," I say in a quiet, yet firm voice. "Please tell me you didn't." Another shrug by Mr. Illegal Substance Experimenting extraordinaire. "Ian!" I glare at him. "Listen, this was the first and last time you will ever do this! You scare me. This is just the beginning, and you're already taking the 'celebrity' lifestyle cliché to the extreme. You are better than this." My voice weakens with concern.

As Ian opens his mouth to speak, a restless sigh surprises us, drawing our attention to the back of the room. Daniel shakes his head, seeming as far from pleased as possible as he pushes himself off the wall. "For fuck's sake," he murmurs unfolding his arms from his chest. He gives Ian a look that makes the three of us flinch in unison. "Let's go grab a beer."

Both Tasha's and my eyes grow while Ian's lips twitch. "Daniel Stark, did you just ask me out?" Ian says, his voice tinged with mischief and a smear of sleaze. "O . . . M . . . G, I just died all dies!"

I swear Daniel looks like he is about to deprive Ian of dear life. *Yeah, rattle that cage why don't you, gorgeous? Life's overrated anyhow.*

Daniel expels a rush of air. "Just grab your shit and let's go."

Ian's joking pretense wanes once he sends me a hesitant glance. I nod, signaling I'm not sure what it's all about, but what I'm sure of is that he means well, always.

As Ian collects his phone and wallet from the low table, and Daniel takes a few silent steps to reach me. He leans in to leave a soft kiss on my lips, "I won't be late."

Tasha and I watch the odd duo as they make their way to the indoor garage. Tasha wrinkles her brows, and I shrug in response.

"What in the heavens was that all about?" She puts our mutual thoughts into words. "Though, if there's anyone who can get some sense into Ian's head," she murmurs

I shake my head in bewilderment. "He never ceases to surprise me."

"Well, I must say that lately your fiancé hasn't failed to

surprise me either."

"What do you mean?" My head snaps her way.

"In a good way." Tasha spreads her arms to the sides in feigned defense. "The last interview he gave . . . I don't think that there are any females at Stark Software that don't have a major crush on your soon-to-be Mr. Hayley Grace. More now than ever."

Noticing my perplexed expression, Tasha says, "About only investing in companies that have women founders?"

I shake my head, inwardly frowning over Daniel's severe condition of never-dishing-the-ever-loving-love-out.

Tasha reaches for her phone, manicured fingers working the screen. "Here, read this." She hands me her cell.

Daniel Stark, a San Francisco-based tycoon and the CEO of Stark Software Inc., made a gallant announcement last week at the FP&A for Hi-tech Summit that he'd only consider investing in startups with at least one female founder.

Stark explained his brave decision. "It is often that female entrepreneurs find it more challenging to secure funding or get their concepts across. They don't fit the typical mold of the business/ hi-tech world entrepreneurs." Stark added, "They are not men."

Stark distinguishes that diversity in business is a good thing and pointed out that that's exactly what women bring to the game. "Women entrepreneurs are more likely to work toward measured, profitable growth with fairly little interest in just positioning themselves for the beneficial exit," Stark said, referring to the latest study by the *Organization of Entrepreneurs* suggesting women make better entrepreneurs than men.

D, you are simply beyond . . .

Tasha observes me for a beat and smirks. "Exactly!"

· · ·

I place my sketching pad face down on the bed to the sound of the en suite door opening. Folding my legs under me, I gaze up at Daniel toweling his hair dry. He is in a pair of boxer briefs, his wide, tanned chest is still damp from the shower. Daniel came back about an hour after Tasha left. I was on the phone with my parents when he kissed my cheek and mouthed that he was going to take a quick shower.

"What?" he says with a light chuckle to my more than overt ogling as he continues to towel his hair. He drops the towel to his neck, his hair sticking out in a sexy mess.

"Did you have a nice evening?" I shamelessly run my eyes over him. "Y'all got some mani-pedi action? Matching tattoos after?" I tease and get an adorable eye roll in response. "So, um, what did you talk to Ian about?"

"Just told him that he'll be on the fast track to send everything he's got to hell if he continues to act like a reckless adolescent." Daniel sends the towel flying into the bathroom and drops to the bed beside me.

I look at him prone, his head rested on his folded arms. "You were worried about him," I say softly.

"You're important to me. He is important to you." Simple. Very simple. *It's that thing you do, D. You just blow me away, time after time.*

Daniel shifts to his side, resting his head on his elbow. His eyes follow me as I mirror him.

"Do you think he listened to you?" I take his free hand in mine and bring it to my lips.

"I hope he did."

I tip my head up, looking at his handsome face. "Thank you for doing this. I love you."

He sends his hand to my waist, pulling me closer to him. We lie facing each other, a sliver of air between us. Daniel leans in to kiss my lips, and not long after, he shows me with indulging, gentle, and passionate gestures just how much he loves me too.

Before switching the light off, I give Daniel's pensive expression another quick glance. He's done it again; shortly after making the sweetest love to me, he disappeared inside his own head. The graveness that veils his face leaves me restless. It doesn't seem like his usual introspections about work, or whatever usually occupies his mind. There's something new, something that seems to torment him. I place a soft kiss on his chest, snuggling deeper under his embrace.

"Good night, Hales." He kisses my hair.

"D, are you okay?" I whisper. Really meaning, please talk to me. Whatever it is, I'm here for you.

"I have you in my arms, baby. I'm okay."

Chapter 9: When Birds Sing Off-Key

The bright side about drowning in work is it takes your mind off things. Off the niggling feeling at the back of your mind that something is coming over the man you love. Off the fact that over four weeks have passed since your last period. Off stopping you from marching to the nearest pharmacy and buying a truckload of home pregnancy tests. Off freaking the hell out about what life has in store for you. Off one of your besties playing with lethal fire.

"Knock, knock." Josh's ocular hazard smile illuminates my cubicle before the rest of his preppy being materializes.

I take a drink of my half-drunk, lukewarm coffee, wince, and put the cup back on the desk. "Is this a 'who's there' thing?"

Josh shakes his head with a rather toned down grin. "More along the lines of have coffee with me at the Starbucks around the corner?"

Coffee in a neutral, non-business-esque territory, boss? My crystal ball predicts a girl talk in my near future. The short walk to the coffee shop strikes me odd, given Josh's line of topics that vary from the weather to domesticated cats. Seems like he's having a hard time calibrating what's really on his mind. I collaborate, discussing the bland topics, giving him the time he needs to open up.

I take another drink of my oh-so-welcomed double shot, extra hot, Grande cappuccino listening to Josh as he tells me about my Ian's recent controversial, to be putting it mildly, behavior. No matter how long they've been dating, each time I think about it, it still takes me a moment and a half to make sense of the whole Josh and Ian legitimate couple thing. The classic tale of Ken doll and Cruella de Vil playing house.

Josh sighs, his shoulders collapsing in perfect harmony with his sinking features. I perk up to the change in his casual demeanor. "Thing is," he says. "I knew full well what I was getting myself into when we started seeing each other. I never expected it to be . . . easy."

So it's an Ian issue he wanted to talk to me about.

"But I think . . ." He sighs again. "I-I think I'm way over my head here." My features furrow. He shakes his head solemnly. "I'm afraid he doesn't know how to cope with everything that's happening to him lately and he's taking it out on our relationship. Especially after that talk he had with his mom."

"Hold on, what talk with his mom?"

Josh appears genuinely surprised by my question. "Didn't he tell you? I thought he told you and Tasha everything."

I shake my head, somewhat offended.

"His mom called him when he came back from New York right after the movie's cast was announced. She totally disparaged him, Hayley. Told him he should be ashamed of himself for linking his family's name to such degrading public exposure." Josh's cheeks flush with anger. "Their son is about to fulfill his lifelong dream and what do they do? Tarnish it! And I guess you know how he gets whenever they manage to belittle him just a little more."

I push my coffee mug aside; there's already too much bitterness inside me. I'm not a hater, but I have nothing even remotely amicable in my heart for Ian's parents. His father especially. He's the mastermind behind making Ian feel like shit grand mission. His mother is usually the one taking orders. Unfortunately, she tends to execute them fairly well too.

"Don't give up on him so quickly. I know just how important you are to him." My eyes challenge Josh, asking him to prove Ian is better than that.

"I'm not. I won't," he says somberly. "But I can only take so much, Hayley. Some things I won't be able to overlook." We both know exactly what he means. And frankly, I'd never expect him to. There are lines one should never cross when in a serious relationship.

I nod and squeeze his hand over the table.

"This is as unprofessional as I've ever been," he says, defeated. "But I love him. I don't want to let him go."

Back at my desk, before shooting Tash and Ian a message ordering them both to meet me for drinks after work, I send a glance toward Josh's office. He's one of the good guys. I hope my Ian realizes that before it's too late.

. . .

We each hold one of Ian's hands over the tall, round table. Tasha seated on a high stool with a bottle-green sheath dress on and a cucumber Martini by her side. Me with a sweating glass of water. And Ian, feigning indifference, eyeing his Caipirinha, clearly avoiding our eyes.

"So how you doing, handsome?" I say, encouraging Ian to finally award me with a glance.

"Even the fucking birds in my skies sing off-key." He snorts a chuckle. "What's up with the grieving vibe? Smile, gorgeous ladies. Everything's peaches and cream." He studies us with a smile that slowly turns flat.

"So what did your parents say about the big news?" Tasha asks.

Vicious much, missy? I flinch. Talk about ripping off the Band-Aid.

Ian's mask drops, revealing his pain. He retrieves his hands from our hold and takes a long drink of his glass. "They asked me to drop the movie." He takes another generous swig, seeming emotionally bankrupt.

Tasha and I exchange a let's-get-rid-of-them-and-hide-the-evidence stare.

"Hey." I rest my hand on his bicep. "Screw them, Ian. Really, if your happiness means nothing to them, then they shouldn't count."

"I was raised with the belief that family is above all, and I strongly believe that," Tasha says, holding Ian's gaze. "But when it comes to yours, I'm sorry, but I think it's time you cut them loose."

I nod in complete agreement. They just keep on hurting him. Time after time.

"And while you figure out what you want to do or soak in your newfound stardom," I say and am rewarded with a beautiful, naughty Ian smile. "Please don't do anything you'll regret later. Anything that you won't be able to undo." Ian's gaze takes a firmer edge. "Josh loves you," I add, my voice just above a whisper.

For a silent while, we sip our drinks in a contemplative state.

"Do you think that anal is the new black?" Tash asks. I almost choke on my next sip and Ian comes to life. "You know how I love my romance, right?" We both nod, well familiar with Tasha's insatiable appetite for romance novels. "It seems like 'pop my backside cherry' is the new hot thing. For a long time, it was the virgin gets deflowered, unleashes her inner cheetah, and becomes an immediate sex goddess theme." Ian and I crack a smile at the same time. "But lately, it's like the one precious thing you share with your love object is letting him access your backdoor."

Ian lets out a free chuckle. "Letting him access your backdoor, really, miss prissy? I think we're out of the playpen, it's A-okay for you to say you want to be fucked up the –"

"We got it," I say, raising my hand.

"Have you ever tried it, anal?" Ian asks, his entire face smiling.

Before he is able to finish his sentence, Tasha cuts him off. "No." She scowls. "The last person who asked me, I asked him if it was okay if I return the favor with a strap-on. *Huge surprise*, the issue was dropped."

"Rafa?" Ian's lips rise up in obscenity. Tasha's glare makes him turn my way. He smirks at me, the question seconds from leaving his mouth. I give him a hostile look to which he physically withdraws, saying, "Don't give me that look. I sometimes have nightmares of that look."

. . .

"Drive safe." Ian closes Tasha's car door. She rolls down the window to say good-bye. In succession, we both squat down to place noisy smooches on her cheek. When Tasha's headlights fade out, Ian sees me to my car.

"I want you happy," I tell him, taking his hand in mine. We swing our joined hands, walking the last few steps to my car.

"I am. Really." Ian's voice morphs thoughtful. "It's just; it's time I stop taking their shit."

"I agree." I nod. Beeping my car open, I turn to hug my Ian.

He squeezes me tightly, his lips descending to my hair.

Keeping me in his embrace for a while longer, he whispers in my ear, "Daniel's a great guy. That pep talk he gave me the other day . . . He's cool."

I ease back from our embrace. "I know. I love you." I send him a soft smile. "Please don't hurt yourself." He pulls me into a warm, tight hug, telling me good night.

I don't even make it out of the parking lot when a text message lands in my phone. I roll to a stop and read the message.

Ian: Daniel is cool. Oh, and not to mention, he's fuckable in magnificent and awe-inspiring proportions.

I step on the gas. The amused headshake that follows is uncontrollable.

Chapter 10: Don't Rain on My Parade

"Hey, where do you think you're going?" A firm, large hand traps mine, stopping me from getting out of bed.

I turn to a luscious sight of a semi-awake Daniel. "Getting ready for work."

"Um, I don't think so." Daniel's morning voice, this bass-coated voice with enough hoarseness that strums just the right chords in me.

"Is that so?" I run my eyes over his toned chest and that heart-racing crooked smile of his.

"C'mere you." And I'm pulled back into our warm bed.

I feign seriousness, trying hard to wipe off the smile blooming on my lips. "I need to be at the office in thirty." My words fall on deaf ears, albeit a very attentive mouth. "I really . . ." I say futilely trying to wiggle out from under the divinely mass of man above me. "I-I, oh God."

"You were saying?" Daniel murmurs to the heated skin between my thighs.

Threading my fingers into his morning hair, I close my eyes. "Daniel." His name together with my resentment leaves my lips on a breath. I pull his head closer to me, inhabitations melting away by desire.

Gazing at me with predatory eyes as I'm reeling from my ecstasy, Daniel says, "Stunning." With the right amount of roughness, he flips me to my stomach, propping me on my knees before him. He teases me till I push against him in a plea, and with one fluid thrust, he fills me in the most delicious way. Daniel's hands come up to grip my hips as he works his body to pleasure us both. Sounds of our drunken pleasure fill the room, matching our rhythm as it picks up. I push against him as he thrusts into me with great abandon until we're both lying side by side, spent and blissfully sated.

"Hey," I say, retracing Daniel's chest with the pad of my finger, trailing up to the spiral tattoo on his shoulder. "Why didn't you tell me about your new investment approach?"

His features edge. "It's just another thing we're exploring these days." As ever, Daniel downplays his generosity and benevolence. Turning to lie on my side, my head resting on my elbow, I look at him. His humbleness is one of his most attractive virtues. One of so many. Sensing my stare on him, he turns his head on the pillow to look at me.

"It's an admirable thing to do."

He shrugs. "Unfortunately, men have it easier raising funds. I just thought some balance was missing. Especially with the great ideas and innovation the women bring to the table." His eyes soften. "The two most important people in my life are women. Incredible ones." A gentle smile takes over my lips. For a brief beat, Daniel's thoughts, once again, turn him somber. Before I'm able to comment, he shakes it off and turns back to me, this time with a suggestive, crooked smile. "Ready for round two?"

"You'll get me sacked." I jump out of bed. I know better than to let him try to seduce me.

"Sucking sounds just as good," Daniel says, humor lacing his words.

I take a step back, shaking my head. "I already had to cancel a meeting. Seriously, I'll get fired." I blow him a kiss over my shoulder and scurry to the bathroom.

"Good, maybe then you'll finally do something about your illustrations," he calls after me.

. . .

Driving, I sing along to The Dunwells, loudly and ridiculously out-of-tune, smiling at the world. The effect of a Daniel-infused morning. With an intense caffeine craving, I check the time on the control display. I have more than twenty minutes before my next meeting. Just enough time for a quick stop at the nearest coffee place. Looking for a parking space, I put together a short list of perfect beverages to quench my cravings. Hazelnut and Caramel Ribbon Crunch Frappaccinos are head to head by the time I make my way to the archangel that's smiling at me, the tall, head-to-toe black-clad barista.

Stepping out of the sacred caffeine establishment, I take the first sip of my drink. Closing my eyes, I wait for the sweet, creamy pleasure to reach all the way up the straw, right into my waiting mouth. The moan I let out next should be rated PG13. The little things that can make a girl nearly climax. I don't let my hollering phone kill the moment and let it go to voicemail. Whoever it is can wait for five minutes. This drink is all I can focus on right now.

Passing a few cars, I make my way to mine and admire the brightness of the day. Snippets from earlier this morning flash before my eyes, adding some rosiness to my overall beaming. Daniel above me, hazel eyes wild with desire, sweat beads forming above a scarred brow, full lips hovering next to mine. With a silly smile, I let myself get carried away to the little porny world my mind is orchestrating.

"Hayley Grace?" A voice brutally bursts my scrumptious bubble.

Startled, I raise my eyes, the straw still held between my lips. A guy in a light blue blazer, brown corduroys, a trimmed beard, and a combed back 'do, complete with the essential thick rim, plastic spectacles, smiles at me. My brows crease as I try to search my memory for any recollection of him. Nothing about the hipsterism epidemic victim rings familiar.

"Miss Grace." He extends his leather bracelet adorned hand for a shake. "Can I call you Hayley?"

"Depends," I say, giving him another overt examination. "I don't think we've met before."

He chuckles lightly. "No, we haven't." His hand still hanging between us, waiting. "Byron, Byron Hobson." I send a hesitant hand to meet his. "Of *Celebrity Gabfest*," he adds.

I jerk my hand back as though I just touched scorching curling iron. Sensing the forthcoming turbulence in my force field, I let my hand drop to my side and shake my head. "Oh, no. Whatever it is, the answer is no." I'd rather have a thousand leeches suck my body cold than talk to any media parasite. *Never again.*

"Hey, hold up, Hayley." He hastens his pace to match mine. "Just a quick chat. Did you guys set a date yet?" His face is a display of amicable cajolery.

Giving him a second side-glance, I raise a hand, signaling for him to stop right where he is. "Have a nice day, Byron Hobson," I say and point the remote at my car, beeping it open. With my drink in one hand, I hurry to open the door with the other.

"Hayley." My stalker's harsh tone demands my attention.

I throw my purse into the passenger seat and crane my neck over my shoulder.

His smile slowly crooks into a malevolent warning, one that I fail to arm myself against. "Are you going to raise the child together?"

I spin back to fully face him, my eyes wide open. How in the hell does he know about our plans? I just gape at him, a foolish, disconcerting smile frozen on my face. I'm too stunned for my vocal cords to catch up with the questions in my head.

His frame-rimmed eyes join his disturbing smile. "Or is it true, is Daniel Stark indeed leaving you for Robin and their child?"

I blink at him. And blink again. As though he just spoke in a foreign language. My mind works to translate the wording. I remain unmoving. *Keep cool, Hayley.* It's not the first time; there's always something on Daniel in the media, and it's mostly well-fabricated nonsense. Or a very creative twist of the truth. I take a bothered breath. Queasy, I duck into the car. With frenzied taps on the lock pin, I bolt myself in the safe confines of my vehicle. Checking the rearview mirror, I follow the tabloid journo as he tucks his hands into his pockets and shrugs. His lips set into a pursed, narrow constriction, appearing to whistle as he turns on his heels.

My eyes drop to the cold drink wedged between my thighs while my stomach attempts to keep what I've managed to consume so far in. The thing about spiteful, yellow journalism, even though you clearly know that it is what it is – "yellow" – ignoring it is easier said than done. The words "leaving you, Robin, and their child" keep smarting in my head, repeatedly, like some psychedelic hypnoses. And I do something that I know I shouldn't do. At least not before talking to Daniel and finding out what it's really all about. I get my phone out of my purse and type: Daniel Stark, Robin, Child into the search engine.

The first headline that catches my eyes manages to empty my

lungs of oxygen. The photo of the beautiful redhead further down the page assaults my stomach like a nasty punch. I skim through the content. ". . . of course, I would like the father of my child to be a part of his life. I know he is in a relationship, but it has never before affected our long and strong friendship." My heart drums in my ears as I try to digest what I've just read. I look at the image of the elegant redhead in the A-line dress and it feels like the image burns into my eyes. *This Robin person is pregnant with Daniel's child? They are friends? This is insane.*

I'm uncertain how much time passes till I'm able to unglue my eyes from the photo. I need to shake it all off before driving to work and actually beginning this day. I shouldn't let this thing evolve into something it might not be. Probably isn't. I take a deep breath, doing my very best not to freak the hell out, jump to conclusions, or drive home, pack my things, and move out. This would never happen. Daniel would never be unfaithful. He'd never sleep with someone else. *Never. Except for the one time, he did . . .*

I start the car and slowly roll it to the nearest trashcan where I bring it to a stop again. Stepping out, I chuck my drink with a great vengeance into the can. A splash of liquid mocha sloshes back out, missing me by an inch.

The pulse in my head turns into a migraine by the time my first meeting finishes. The rest of the day passes with me policing myself not to go through the rabbit hole that is gossip websites or call Daniel and confronting him.

Chapter 11: Fait Accompli

The jingle of keys coming in contact with the glass bowl shakes me out of my brief bubble of contradictions. Daniel's voice, speaking to someone on the phone, echoes from the living room. I give myself a quick peek in the mirror, agitated, running a hand over my loose waves, and switch the light off.

I make my way to the living room. Needless to say, I'm one tight spring of edginess and apprehension. Earlier today, I decided to find out what's really going on over a face-to-face conversation. Color me conservative, but I don't think that a, "So hey, have you knocked up someone else lately?" is the kind of conversation one should have over the phone with her significant other. And since we haven't talked thus far, I had the entire day to try not to obsess too much over my morning's encounter, and not to come up with the worst scenarios. The "try not to" part didn't work too well.

Noticing me entering the living room, Daniel closes the distance between us. Still on the phone, he bows to kiss my lips. He gives my waist a small squeeze and passes by me, unbuttoning his shirt en route to the hall. I follow him to the bedroom, glaring at his back fairly astonished by his inability to read the blizzard in my eyes. Seems like the only time men are really in-tune with our emotions is when we emit pheromones into the air.

Finishing his call, he drops the phone on the bed and resumes unbuttoning his shirt.

"So how was your day?" I say.

With his fingers still working the last button, his eyes lift to mine. His special smile comes before he answers. "It was. Yours?"

At their own volition, my arms wrap around my waist. I stare at him, taking an inward "try to bridle all the crazy" inhale and tread forward with caution. "Everything's fine?"

I'm not certain if my eyes are playing tricks on me, or it's just my overloaded distressed mind, but for a fleeting moment, he appears distraught. When his eyebrows rise in question and in tandem to his arms folding over his chest, said worry I thought I might have noticed is gone. "Yeah. What is it, Hales?" His demeanor may transmit confidence and nonchalance. However, the tick of the muscle above his jaw tells me otherwise.

"Funny, earlier today I was asked whether you're going to have a child . . ." His eyes hone in on mine, his features hardening. "With someone called Robin, and whether you are leaving me. So I'm a bit curious, you see." True or not as this might be, every word leaving my mouth is a stab in my stomach. Together, they feel like a merciless slaughter.

"I'd never leave you." Curt and fierce. Not the answer I was hoping for, though. Denial would have worked better here. He takes a step toward me. I hug my waist tighter, defensive.

"Daniel." His name scrapes out of my lips. "What's going on?"

"It's nothing." He takes another step. Reflexively, I signal for him to stop. "I didn't want you involved in this." He shakes his head, cursing under his breath.

My hand drops to my chest because, all of a sudden, it's a little hard to breathe. "Involved in what exactly?" Uncontrolled, my voice is a few octaves higher. *There's smoke, there's fire.*

"Fuck's sake." He inhales through his nose. "Hales, baby, believe me when I say, you should not be involved in this. *It's nothing.*"

"Can you stop for a second?" My quills stand at attention. "What in the hell is going on?" My eyes bore into his. "What shouldn't I be involved in exactly?"

He lets out a frustrated sigh. "Some gold-digger claims I'm the father of her child." Daniel's face stones over while his eyes take a quest to disclose what goes on in my mind.

"Why would she even say, claim, something like that? Did you ... D-Does she have, ah, anything to base it on?" I desperately wish I could close my eyes and erase seeing the flinch across his face I just witnessed. My body tightens as though preparing for the impending punch.

"It's that woman I—the one I was with when we broke up." He takes a step toward me, and I take an involuntary one back. "Hales, I promise you nothing's there but an attempt to get some money, or publicity, or I don't know what."

"How can you be so sure? W-what if she's really pregnant?" I blink at him, the words leaving my mouth tasting bitterly surreal. This can't be happening. Not now, not when we're ... It's supposed to be our child. I feel sick.

"It's not mine, Hayley. It's all about money." His answer comes out coated with irritation.

"How do you know? How can you be so sure? What if you're wrong?" My eyes hold his, shooting unspoken warnings. I lift my hand. "Daniel, I wear this ring because I am planning to marry you someday. I want to know what I'm in for." The intensity of our locked stare is about to spark by shorting. *"Not that it would make me change my mind.* But what if you have a child out there? What kind of a man, person, would it make you not to at least find out?"

His teeth graze his bottom lip repeatedly, his eyes narrowed at me. "It's not mine, Hayley. You want me to go into details? I was covered when we . . ."

I close my eyes. The content of my stomach shooting up my throat. I open them, giving him a hard look. "You can't be sure! This is not a gut feeling situation." I raise my voice. "Accidents happen! It's something you have to find out." I've long abandoned my attempt at keeping myself composed.

Daniel's eyes morph from riled to majorly pissed. "You know what, if it's so important to you, I'll have a goddamn paternity test." His voice takes a louder, rougher tone. "Find out if by any miracle I'm the goddamn incarnation of the Holy Spirit and have impregnated this woman!" He takes another step and finally reaches me. Daniel sends his hand to my forearm. My physical response as I jolt back from his touch leaves us both in momentary shock. I give him another muddled look and turn to leave. My fleeting defense mechanism goes into gear. Not really knowing what I'm doing or where I'm going. Daniel follows me out of the room.

"Hales, if you are running away again, I . . ."

I spin to face him. "You're what, Daniel?"

He closes his eyes, hanging his head down. He takes a deep breath and looks up at me. His voice lowers as he says, "If you think for a second I'm letting you run away again . . . We're way past this."

His words sober me up. "I'm not going anywhere." *My* words almost a whisper. I look behind him at some indistinct point on the wall. "Some masochistic part of me wants you to walk me through that night."

"Don't." He shakes his head. "How did we even end up here?" comes an exhausted murmur.

My livid stare darts to him. "What can I say? What led us to this point, Daniel? Well, your successful endeavor is hard to erase given it is shoved in my face in the form of a *child*." It's safe to say, my irritation with the situation is back.

"Alleged child, for fuck's sake. Can you not be that girlfriend now, Hayley?" He echoes my gaze.

Angry fire licks all the way up from my belly to my mouth. "For fuck's sake, Daniel, which girlfriend? The one that feels sick to her stomach thinking about you screwing someone else? Oh, I'm sorry for being that kind of . . . *fi-an-cée*." I lean on the hall's wall, needing space. Needing to calm the heat storm gathering velocity in me. Needing badly for everything to be a bad joke.

Daniel mirrors me, leaning on the opposite wall. "No, the one that brings back something we agreed to bury a long time ago and starts a shitfest about it."

"I can't believe you sometimes," I snap.

"It's you I can't believe sometimes." Daniel spreads his hands to his sides in frustration. "Christ Hayley, I . . . Can . . . Not . . . Rewrite . . . Our . . . History." Silence falls between us after Daniel's last words dissolve into the fury, confusion and multitude of uncertainties we're sharing. "Why are we fighting?" His voice is softer. His head leaning on the gray wall, his eyes on mine. Weary.

"We aren't." An unbidden tear rolls down my cheek.

Daniel pushes himself from the wall with a start. With one hurried step, he's cupping my face, his eyes soulful. In a tender, worried voice he says, "Hales, you're crying."

Something about his concern, the candor of his voice, the look in his eyes that can never be more caring, brings me to burrow under his arms. Pressing my face to the hard planes of his chest, I let him hug my bruised ego and heart. "I'm not crying; it's just stupid liquid frustration," I murmur under my breath.

Daniel lets me be, embracing me tight, pressing soft kisses on the center of my head. Wordlessly, he slides to the floor, taking me with him. Until he is leaning on the wall with me cuddled under his arm.

For a long beat, we stare at each other, processing. Daniel brushes a lock of hair over my shoulder. His hand comes back to rest on my chest, his finger retracing my collarbone. "I didn't want you involved because I knew just how upset it would make you. That's why I didn't tell you. I have people working on it." He takes a silent breath. "I'm not sure how it started circulating. It's hard to keep these kinds of things under control when the other party is trying to do the exact opposite. For the money, publicity, or God knows what."

I just stare at him, listening to his voice. I've lost the will to talk about it any longer. I'm left with a sense of bitterness that's soaring around my heart.

"Have the paternity test," I say with an exhausted sigh.

"I will if that's what you want."

"You should want it too. You need to know." Jekyll is definitely fighting Hyde and whatever was about to come out of Daniel's lips remains unsaid. The next words to leave *my* mouth jostle my insides before they meet air. "The articles online said that the two of you are friends. That, that's what Rob – what she said." I can't even bring myself to say her name.

Daniel closes his eyes for a stretch. "Baby, we met once. There wasn't much talking. We've never met after that. I didn't even know her name before Brian, my PR guy, told me about it. There was never anything cordial between that woman and me, let alone any sort of friendship."

"I believe you," I say in a dainty voice.

His eyes grow softer. "I love you. I'm sorry you have to go through this."

I rest my face on his chest, closing my eyes. Daniel wraps his arms around me, holding me in his embrace till evening washes the house in darkness.

Chapter 12: Knowledge is Not Always Power

"You ready?" Tasha asks as she settles herself on one of the kitchen's highchairs. Green eyes perfectly lined 70's-style run over me. Her mid-forehead bangs slightly sway from side to side as she concludes her assessment with a tilt of her head. "Sure?"

I roll my eyes. "Out with it already."

Tasha shifts her pencil skirt clad bottom on the chair, and with much unnecessary drama, she turns to open her thin notebook. In unison, both our faces adhere to the screen for some good ol' self-flagellation. Green attentive eyes examine every angle of the woman in the tight navy dress that showcases a notable baby bump, while mine are cemented to the face, studying it fastidiously in sheer masochism. *Yet again.* It's a new interview with *the* redhead. She's really cashing in on her childbearing situation.

"Humm," Tasha wrinkles her nose. "She's, she's . . ."

"Pretty?" I raise my stare from the screen. "Elegant. Normal? Everything you don't want someone like her to look like?"

"I was about to say that that red looks like it came out of a bottle." She wrinkles her nose again, this time with a twist of a mouth.

"She's an event planner," I add. Somewhere between the lines, the pictures tell us both that she doesn't look like some bimbo gold-digger. She seems completely ordinary, pretty and ordinary and so much more. She looks like the kind of women who'll wait for the other side to make the first move. A notion that makes me want to retch all over the screen. It's not okay to feel such healthy hatred toward someone you've never met. *But apparently, someone who had the pleasure of meeting your boyfriend's penis.*

"She looks like someone who has better places to go in the afterlife," Tasha deadpans. My lips pull up. Gotta love my besties. If someone is, God forbid, out to hurt me, he has no place in this world.

"What are we looking at?" Ian says, coming back into the kitchen, buttoning his jeans.

"You could have done that in the bathroom," Tasha scolds, pointing at his fly.

Ian shrugs it off and wedges himself between us, looking at the screen. "Who's Little Red Riding Ho?"

Tasha and I snort in stereo.

"The alleged sperm robber," Tasha fills in with a nod.

Ian's hand sneaks in from behind Tasha and me, slamming the screen shut. "No!" Fazed, we turn Ian's way. "No! Enough. I'm not letting you sit here and gobble up shit that will start a crapfest in your gorgeous head." He taps my head with his finger. "Seriously, why do you need to know who she is, how she looks, or what she does? What good will it do you?"

Tasha traps her lip between her teeth, bobbing her head in agreement. "Sorry. He's right."

"Nu-uh." Ian smacks my hand just before it reaches the laptop. "Leave the vile device alone!"

I narrow my eyes at the vile device. *Later . . .*

"Oh no, so help me, my little glutton for punishment." He shakes his finger at me. "If you even get close to a damn browser." Ian's stare is even sharper than the one I'm deflecting. "*Now*, I need a drink."

I slide my glass his way to be rewarded with a semi-shocked, wide-eyed glare. "What?" I say.

"Take this germ-populated thing away from me." He waves his hand at the glass.

"Oh, I almost forgot about Mr. sterile and his drinking from other people's cups phobia." I throw my eyes up.

"Oh, right," Tasha's nostrils flare. She gives Ian the evil eye. "Drinking from someone's cup is a big no-no, but jumping from one erect penis to another is A-okay!"

Ian, being Ian, answers with, "I only wish I could actually be actively pollinating."

Tasha opens her mouth, ready to speak, but shuts right back as I barge in. "You know what, *you just stop*. Just stop it right now. It's not funny anymore. If you don't want to be in a relationship, and you miss sleeping around so much, break it off with Josh. Otherwise, just stop with these tactless comments."

Silence.

A silence charged with surprise dawns on us. Both Tasha and Ian's heads slowly pivot my way. I wince, being on the receiving side of their stares. I swallow hard witnessing their troublesome stare exchange.

"Okaaay," Ian says, widening his stare. In succession, Tasha pulls her purse up over her shoulder, and Ian shoves his wallet into his back pocket. Their next words collide as they finally speak.

"We're going for drinks," Tasha.

"Shopping, now!" Ian.

Not a beat passes before each of my friends grabs one of my arms and together lead me toward the front door.

. . .

"I meant what I said," Ian says, squeezing my hand. "Before, about obsessing over this shit you're going through." His expression mellows. I bring the thin straw of my drink to my lips and take a sip.

When Tasha left us earlier with so many shopping bags in her hands, I thought she'd topple over, Ian and I spontaneously decided to grab a drink together before parting ways for the night.

"It's just," I huff. "Not only that I have to relive this . . ." I wave my hand in the air. "Thing. This time, it's with the rest of humanity. The tabloids can't get enough of this story."

Ian's eyes run over my fallen face. "Worst-case scenario, what would you do?" he says.

"What are you asking exactly?"

"What if she's indeed pregnant with Daniel's child?" This question, especially coming from Ian's lips, guts me. "Would you leave him?"

"No. It would probably kill me a hundred times, but I don't think I'll ever leave him voluntarily."

Ian bobs his head, excepting my answer. "Then you should, just like I said before, keep yourself away from anything that will hurt you. Stay under the radar till it's sorted out."

"God Ian, I can't even. I just wish it would all go away."

Ian threads his fingers with mine and leans in to press a kiss to my cheek. "Whatever it is, I'm always here for you."

"Same here. And *I* meant what *I* said earlier." I search his eyes. "If you have any doubts, break it off with Josh."

His shoulders collapse as he turns to take another taste of his drink. "I don't have any doubts about Josh. It's the timing that sucks."

"Really?" I say. "So when you're happy and fulfilling your dream it's not the right time to be with him?"

He grimaces. "That's not what I meant, Hales."

"I'm just saying; he's crazy about you, so don't hurt him or yourself."

The patriotic tune coming from my phone breaks our tense moment. "It's Tash," I tell Ian, looking at the screen.

"Let me," Ian says, taking the device from my hand. "What up, Barbie?" He listens and winces. "Oh shit." I study him as he listens to Tasha, my brows almost meeting. "Hang on, Tash, let me check with Hales." He faces me. "Um, did you talk to your parents?"

My parents? My head jerks back in surprise. "What about?"

"Gorgeous, the shit's all over the internet."

Oh. *Oh, crap.* I flinch. I'm sure the dread expanding inside me is written all over my face.

"Precisely," Ian says, confirming his assumption.

I can't help but wonder if my beloved father had already put out a hit on my beloved fiancé. Yes, he probably has. Or worse, he's decided to go the DIY route. *Note to self: remind dad of the importance of the Ten Commandments, especially the "thou shalt not kill" one.*

Chapter 13: Into the Woods

Daniel: Jeans and comfortable shoes. Pick you up at seven.

I tilt my head, rereading the odd text on my phone. *What the what?*

Should I be standing at attention while waiting?

Daniel: Seven.

How Daniel of you. Why yes, Sir, go ahead and give out your orders. After all, we're all here at your beck and call. This is ridiculous. It might have worked for him in the past. Not anymore. I speed dial his number. *My number one.*

"Hales, anything urgent? I'm in a meeting." Authoritative and curt.

I sigh. "Just wanted to ask about that weird message of yours. Never mind."

There's a moment of silence on the line. "Roy, I need to take this one."

"No, Daniel, it's not . . ." *Important.* I sigh again, listening to Daniel telling whoever this Roy person is that he'll call for him in five.

"Hales." He's back.

"You didn't have to –"

"What's up?"

"Where are we going?"

"Somewhere I want to take you."

Now that helped, a lot. My gratitude, Sir.

"What are you up to?" he asks next, glaringly disregarding my initial question.

"I think I should call my parents." I hate bringing this up, but it's out there and should be dealt with, the sooner the better. Unfortunately, there are things that we can't just scrub off. "I hope I'm not too late. I think it's better they hear about Rob . . . her, from me."

"I'll call your dad." Gruff and determined.

"No!" I practically bark the simple word. "Let me. Better I make the call. Daniel, believe me, he'll be less than pleased to hear about it." And by that, I mean he'll probably have your head on a butcher block. Or another part of your body that I'm quite fond of.

"Mr. Stark." It's Anne's voice, Daniel's PA.

"Hales?" Daniel says.

"Go ahead; we'll talk later."

I stare at the phone in my hand. It's time I called my parents. I might as well get it over with already. What could be a better way to spend my lunch break than disappointing my parents? I look around to make sure the cubicles around me are vacant, and just as I'm about to dial, my phone comes to life with "home" flickering on the screen. Home can be either of my parents or both. In this specific moment, I'm opting for my mom.

"Lelly!" I release a trapped breath hearing my mom's comforting voice.

Just as my stiffened psyche mellows down a little, it straightens right back to my dad's voice. "Hayley."

"I was just about to call you guys." I go for casual.

"How are you, sweetheart?" my mom asks.

"I'm fine, Ma. How are you guys? Steven?"

My mom's answer dissipates into my dad's question. "Hayley, is it true?"

It's as if a lead weight just landed on my chest. I feel like I'm twelve again, trapped in my father's solemn gaze as he waits for my answer after asking me whether I've shaved half of Steven's head while he was sleeping. The extenuating circumstances didn't help back then – "but he read my diary, Daddy" – and wouldn't probably in the present case either with "there's a high chance it's not his child, Daddy." I inwardly compose myself and say, "You know how the media is; they always manipulate the truth and take things out of context."

"Hayley, has the man you're engaged to got another woman pregnant?"

I squirm in my chair. A normal person should not be having this conversation with their parents. This is reality show material. "Probably not." Yeah, not much thought behind this quick reply. "It's not what it looks like. This woman is probably after money or publicity."

"Let me get this straight, it's not a complete farce then?" The anger and disappointment in my father's voice is depressing, making my self-conscious grow.

I squirm in my chair once more. "Um . . ." I hesitate, trying to figure out what would be the correct way to make this debacle a tad more palatable.

"Oh Lordy me," my mom breathes in the background.

"Hayley, what can I tell you, I might be old-fashioned, but as I see it, in a healthy relationship, you shouldn't have to worry whether your significant other has allegedly impregnated someone. You don't need to be in such a relationship. For heaven's sake, you need to be with someone who respects you and cherishes everything that you are. Now would be as good a time as ever to get out of this relationship."

Oh, please, Dad, why don't you rip that open wound a little wider? Rub some salt in while you're at it. "Dad, I'm not going to . . ." I'm stopped by the chime of a cell phone coming from the other end.

"The nerve," my father seethes. "I need to answer this one; it's your fiancé." So much disdain in so few words.

Shit!

"No, Dad, don't –" But it's too late.

. . .

"You called my dad?" is how I greet Daniel as he steps into the house. He looks at me from above the two paper bags from some organic store in his hands. My head jerks back in surprise at the odd domestic vision before me. My brows pull in. *D, you went grocery shopping?*

"What did you think?" he asks, bringing me back to my question. "That I'll sit this one out and let you get all the fire?"

"He's not exactly in your favor at the moment," I say, following him to the kitchen.

Daniel sets the bags on the counter and turns to kiss my lips. "He never was." Turning back, he starts getting stuff out of the brown paper bags.

"So what did you talk about?" *Besides the obvious.* My eyes bounce from Daniel to the items he takes out of the bags.

"I tried to explain the situation." He puts a few avocados, some bizarre bags of seeds, and a container of pomegranate juice on the counter. "And then I basically let him bust my balls."

I'm not sure what jars me more, what Daniel just told me, or the odd produce that has assembled on the counter. "You didn't have to do that," I say, taking a step toward him. I send my hand to his waist, pulling at it so he'll turn to face me. Daniel turns and leans his lower back to the counter. I take another step to plant myself between his legs. "Really, you didn't have to do that but thank you." I kiss his jaw.

"It's a fucked-up situation." He sighs and buries his face in my hair. I hug him tight, kissing his chest through his shirt. Taking a lungful of comfort that is his Daniel scent.

"I took the paternity test today."

I slowly trail my eyes up to his. "I didn't know you could have it done before the child was born. She agreed to cooperate?"

"Yes, you can. My lawyer promised her money regardless of the results." Daniel jaw is working under his tanned skin.

"Why?"

"Because I want to leave it behind us as soon as possible."

I hug him tighter. "So do I." Easing off, my eyes land on the peculiar products I almost forgot about. "What have you got here? What's this?" I lift the brown seeds packet, closely inspecting it. *Flaxseed*?

"Things you should be eating while trying to conceive," Daniel says like it's the most natural thing for him to talk about.

My eyes shoot up to his. "How did you even know what one should be eating while . . . ? Daniel Stark, you just up and went to the store?"

His brows furrow. "Yeah."

My lips stretch into a grin. "So you took some time off from running the cyber security world, did some research, and skippity skipped to the nearest organic store?" His confused air turns my grin into a full-blown smile. *Love you so much, D.*

Chapter 14: Forget the World with Me

"Where are we going?" I say, feasting my eyes on Daniel in a gray thermal and jeans as he steers the car onto a dirt road leading to a forest. I watch him under the light coming from the Veyron's console, waiting.

He rolls the car to a stop and turns to me with a hint of a smile, his right hand resting on the wheel. "Camping."

My eyes grow wider to his response. I run them over his face that has taken an amused air. "Okaaay." I linger the word doubtfully. "I'm actually a big fan of our bed," I say. "Just for the record," I add in a murmur.

"Our bed is one of my favorite places on the planet, believe me." His grin morphs wicked. "But I thought a change of scenery would be good for us. Somewhere it could be just you and me, somewhere away from everything . . ." He doesn't complete the sentence, and to be honest, I'm glad he doesn't. Daniel gets out of the car and turns to the backseat to get a couple of backpacks and a bundle of wood logs tied together that I didn't even notice he'd put in the car.

"Wow, you really planned this all out, didn't you?" I say, looking at the gear Daniel has piled on his shoulders. He shrugs and offers me his hand. We walk hand in hand through the woods in pleasant silence till I break it. "I sure hope you got some decent camping food and not that flax-whatever, healthy stuff. I'm starving."

Daniel smiles, turning to me. "Only the best for you."

My eyebrows rise in excitement, encouraging him to divulge the much-anticipated info. "Fine dining, baby. Chili dogs."

"You sure know how to spoil a girl."

He chuckles, tugging on my hand to pull me closer to him. He plants a kiss on my head.

. . .

"D, really, I can help," I say, sitting by the fire, doing absolutely nothing while Daniel starts setting up camp.

He shakes his head. "You watch the food." I inwardly giggle at the thought that crosses my mind. *Me Tarzan, you Jane.*

Clearly, the last thing I do is actually watch the food, for I choose to indulge my eyes on my provider/protector. How can I not when I have Daniel before me all outdoorsy and manly, setting up a place for me to rest my weary head tonight. Daniel squats to stake down the edges of the tent, his features tense in concentration. I need to trap my lips together so, "Hey D, can I trouble that sexy, scarred mouth of yours for a sec, a certain feminine part of my body demands its attention," won't slip out.

"You keep looking at me like that, and we won't have a place to sleep tonight, woman," Daniel says, moving on to the next pole attachment, a light grin playing on his lips as he works to secure it to the ground. Beaming, I rip open a bag of tortilla chips and pop one into my mouth.

With the tent set up, Daniel cleans his hands, patting them on his jeans and bends down to sit next to me. He gives my lips a quick peck and brings a chip to his mouth.

"I think it's ready." I pull one of the foiled hotdogs out of the fire, unfolding the wrapping. "God, it looks amazing." I take a lungful of the sausage, spice, and cheese scent and get the other for Daniel.

"We definitely need to do this more often," Daniel says, polishing a third of his hotdog in one bite.

I take a bite of mine. "Agreed."

Daniel's eyes light up in tandem to his thumb brushing the corner of my mouth. He brings his thumb to his mouth and sucks on the smear of sauce. The way his lips suck on his thumb prompts my creative mind to come up with a couple of fun adult campfire games. Light conversation carries us through our little shindig by the fire.

"Ready for dessert?" Daniel asks, digging through one of the backpacks.

"Always," I say, taking a sip of my soda because, apparently, I've been banned from drinking alcohol till further notice. My reasoning that I'm not even pregnant yet fell on deaf ears. Some fights are just not worth fighting, especially when the other party's sense of reason has a tenuous grasp on logic.

Daniel skewers a couple of marshmallows on a stick and hands it over to me to roast while he turns to break some graham crackers in two, placing a cube of Hershey's on each. I beam at him, only for him to reward me with the sweetest, boyish grin. And at this moment, nothing really matters. It's him and me, and I don't need anything else. Okay, maybe just us and these mouthwatering s'mores. *Daniel and s'mores . . .*

With said thought in mind, I rise to my knees and lean in, sending my tongue to the smudge of chocolate on his lip. "It tastes even better on you," I say to his lips while climbing his thighs. A low groan rumbles from his throat when my determined tongue makes its way to the confines of his warm, sweet mouth. Daniel's hands find their way under my sweatshirt, caressing my skin. I slide forward to graze against his hardened groin. Progressively, our kisses become feverish, sloppy. The heat coming from the fire has nothing on the inferno that is my desire for him. I direct my hands to the hem of his shirt, hurriedly pulling it up over his head. I give him one more scorching kiss and ease back only to kiss a trail over his raspy jaw and down his throat. Daniel's hand reaches the hem of my sweatshirt, pulling it up a little then dropping it back down. He breaks our kiss. My confused stare jumps to his hooded, smoldering eyes.

"Let's take it inside," he says, light flush tinting his sharp cheekbones. "I don't need some horny raccoon getting off on my sexy fiancée."

I burst into laughter. "You didn't just say horny raccoon, did you?"

Daniel snorts, pulling me after him into the tent. In record time, we're both naked inside the sleeping bag. We're still grinning as our lips meet. Daniel turns to lie on me, nudging my legs apart with his thigh. He tips his mouth to brush mine, his tongue coming out to part my lips. He inches back, lightly biting my lips. "Tell me what you want me to do to you." His husky voice timbers all the way inside of me.

My cheeks lightly tint as I bite my lip, returning his intense stare. "I want your mouth on me." My voice comes out hoarse. Hazel eyes become darker as he kisses me next. Wordlessly, he gives me another small kiss and slides down my body. His hands grab my thighs and drop them open. He kisses a trail down one thigh, almost reaching my middle and turns to do the same to my other thigh. My legs quiver as the heat of his mouth comes closer and closer to where I'm wide open and waiting for him.

I cry out, arching my back with the first lapping of his tongue on me. He moves my parted legs to rest on his shoulders and leans in to taste me. Keenly, his mouth works me to a peak, suckling, lapping, and kissing while producing erotic sounds that drive me crazy with lust. I no longer am able to hold myself when he sucks hard on my most sensitive spot, sending warm currents throughout my body. I cry out his name, my eyes shut in ecstasy as my body combusts with pleasure. He keeps his mouth on me till I push his head away because it's too much.

When Daniel lies on top of me this time, it's with an easier pace. And so are his touches, kisses, and thrusts. We hold our stares unbroken under the soft light coming from the bonfire as he moves fluidly on and in me. I tip my chin up, claiming his mouth. He brings his hand to caress my face, his eyes drinking me in. When I tighten around him, he drops his head back, eyes fluttering closed in pleasure. And when his name is ripped out of my lips in utter pleasure, he stiffens in me, releasing his desire with my name in a string of incantations.

"Hales," Daniel says, leisurely tracing his fingers over my naked back.

"Mmm . . ." I murmur, my eyes closed, my head rested on his bare chest.

"Look at me."

I turn to rest my chin on his skin, leveling our stare.

"I need to tell you something." The graveness in his tone has a direct effect on my stomach. "But you need to promise to hear me out first. Promise you'll do that?"

I tense up. "Sure," comes out on a weak chord. My insecurities and dreads standing at attention.

Daniel takes a breath through his nose, his eyes latched to

mine. "I was thinking, perhaps when we get back home tomorrow, I'll move into one of the guest houses . . ."

My eyes grow in distress. "What are you talking about?" shoots out of my mouth.

He places two fingers on my lips. "Hales, hear me out first, please."

My stomach turns viciously, and I can literally feel the blood drain from my face. "I'll move into one of the guest houses, or maybe even to a hotel. I thought maybe until everything clears up, you might want me to stay away. Just for the time being, though I promise you, it's the last thing I want to do. After talking to your dad today, I realized just how this all looks. I can understand his concern. I never wanted you to go through what you must be going through right now. Baby, I'll do whatever you need me to do, even if it means staying away for a while."

I shake my head resolutely, my eyes glazing over. Breathing through the pain of the little piece of my heart he just poked. Another piece of my heart that will always belong to him. "*No*, I don't want you anywhere but close to me, as close as possible. And *no*, I don't want to think things over or wait for things to clear out. *I don't need to.* Because no matter what the consequences are, whatever happens, we'll deal with them together."

Daniel sends his hands to my waist, sliding me up to rest on him, mouth to mouth, heart to heart. "Hales, I swear, you're my everything. Love doesn't even begin to describe what I feel for you."

I press my lips to his, still choked up on his offer. Still raw and vulnerable. Still shaken.

Chapter 15: Just Like an Earthquake

Daniel

I take a lungful, inhaling Hayley's hair again. It's intoxicating. Her smell, the way she feels, her smooth skin, the way *I* feel holding her in my arms. My heart has expanded to capacity. No more space, full of Hales. I'm fucking happily whipped. I press a kiss to her hair, tightening my embrace around her. She can never be close enough. What she told me before falling asleep on my chest is still fresh in my head. "I wish we could be like this more. Just the two of us. Hey, how crazy would it be if we moved to Baja for a while?"

Sounds like a fucking dream. Alas, just like dreams usually end, it's a nice idea to have even if the probability of execution is slim, if at all. I can't just drop everything and go on an infinite vacation. I can't allow myself a long physical distance from the business. I've worked too hard to sit back and watch it crumble. The thought of being in Baja with Hayley does sound damn perfect, though. I let out a sigh. Not viable.

I let these thoughts go. And just like an earthquake, with no warning, the thing that keeps eating at me shakes the surface of the momentary peacefulness. Hayley thinks that the current predicament is an issue. To me, it's nothing but a small, annoying hiccup that hopefully will be left behind us and forgotten once the results arrive. The other thing, though . . . I can't even begin to figure out how to deal with it.

Maybe Baja is not that bad of an idea, after all. At least, for a little while.

Chapter 16: Shake It Off

My eyebrows meet to the muffled noises coming from inside the house. As I take hesitant steps toward our bedroom, my heartbeat accelerates. I worry my lips, confused, not sure what I should do next. It sounds like some sort of a brawl is taking place in the . . . bedroom. Palpable sounds of movements, heavy breathing, the rough graze of heavy furniture taking some serious strain. The voices funneling through the hall dust confusion and a greater part anxiety on my staggered state. Holding my breath, I send my hand to the bedroom's slightly ajar door. I give it a soft push, and in one short-lived moment, my world crashes down.

The room is dimly lit. I narrow my eyes to hone in on the bed first. Long, red, silky hair splayed out on my side of the bed and above it, murmuring sweet nothings, is my Daniel. Bare, strong, and tanned, he fluidly moves above a milky-skinned woman. His lips – the lips that have kissed me more than a million times and promised me forever – passionately kissing someone else. Some things you never, ever want to witness. One of them is watching as the love of your life rip your heart right out of your chest.

"God, yes," cries the breathy feminine voice. She pants and her voice becomes softer as she says, "I'm so happy you're finally mine. I love you."

In hell coma, I flinch at the wail that rips the sensual air, the sharp cry prompting me to search for the source. My knees buckle under me, and I have to hold the doorframe for support. Next to the bed, in a light blue crib, lies the howling commotion. Bundled in a soft, white blanket, he demands his. . .parents' attention. Something clogs my throat, caging in my voice and oxygen. Daniel cranes his neck to look at the crib, meeting my shattered eyes along the way.

"Hales." Comes low and soft.

I shake my head, choking up.

"*Hales*."

Silence.

"Hayley, baby." Somehow, his hand reaches me. "*Hales*."

My eyes rip open in alarm. Instinctively, my body jerks back from Daniel's proximity. Blinking, his concerned features soak in. "Baby, you're okay." Gently, he rests his hand on my cheek. "It was just a dream."

Nightmare, D, of the worst kind.

It takes me a short moment to catalog the surroundings. The tent. The sleeping bag, and the shadows of flames dancing over the thin, fabric walls. I take a deep breath, still tantalized by the vivid dream.

"You okay?" Daniel asks, pulling me closer onto his chest. I bob my head. He pulls me higher for my body to cover his, for his embrace to shield me in. My hastened heartbeat gradually evens out to his steady one. The reminder of earlier this evening lightly washes away the soreness in my chest. I choose not to tell him about my dream, especially with the conversation we had just before falling asleep. The last thing I want is for him to doubt my trust and faith in him, again.

"I'm fine." I kiss his warm neck and burrow deeper into his arms.

Chapter 17: Growing Up?

"There's never an actual right or wrong, gorgeous mine; it's all in the eye of the beholder," Ian says from the other end of the line, sounding ridiculously serious. Justifying why in case he ends up meeting Ricky Martin on his current Hollywood jaunt, Josh should be okay if they hook up.

"You mean in the eye of the reprobate, right?" He chuckles at my jab. "Okay, gotta go, I see Tash," I say, spotting Tasha, who's already sitting next to one of the outside tables in the new Middle Eastern place where we are meeting for lunch.

"'Kay. See you in five." Ian hangs up.

"Hey." I kiss Tasha's cheek before taking a seat next to her. "Looking exceptionally swanky." I admire her soft pink power suit, her hair framing her lightly made-up face in a shiny dark halo.

"I have an important meeting later today."

"Sounds . . . important." I smirk at the menu in my hands.

"It is. I'll tell you guys all about it when Ian gets here."

My eyes climb up above the menu, meeting hers. My brows furrow at her troubled expression. "Do I need an attorney present with me for whatever it is?"

Her head jerks back in surprise. "What?" She seems weighed down by her own thoughts.

"You look like you're about to tell me you've committed a felony." Tasha gives me what appears to be an attempt at a scornful smile that I'm not buying. "Things with Rafa better?" I change the subject for her sake.

"I think so," she says, still not completely with me. "Um, what am I saying? It's actually going pretty well."

"I'm glad for you," I say, letting her be. Whatever it is, she'll tell us when the fizzy part of our trio arrives. Instead, I focus on the description of item twenty on the menu: Maklouba. Meat, rice, spices, fried vegetables. *Hell to the yum.*

"When will you know for sure about the . . . ?" Tasha sets her menu onto the table. I tip my head sideways in question. "About the, um, alleged bastard baby," she elaborates.

I frown. "Bastard baby, really?"

She giggles and shrugs. "For lack of any other suitable word."

I crack a frustrated smile. "Next few days. But," I expel a jaded breath, "can we stay clear of that topic? I'm really trying not to think about it."

"Sure." She squeezes my hand. "Oh, there's Mr. Hollywood."

I look over my shoulder in search of Ian. He smiles back, handsome and stylish in distressed denim overalls, long-sleeved white undershirt, and brown work boots.

Tasha smirks at him, checking out his attire. "Howdy, young Huckleberry."

In lieu of a greeting, Ian drops to his knees before me. His features earnest as he looks up at me. His stare captivates mine while his hand comes up to clasp my knee. My eyes grow wider and fall to his hand on me. "I swear," he breathes audibly, making me bring my eyes back to his. "There's no one else, sweet baby.

My heart, my whole heart, every last piece of it, is completely yours. I've never felt this way before. You're all I can think about day and night." He closes his eyes for a dramatic beat while both Tasha and I gape at him in query.

"The hell?" Tasha peeps.

Ian raises his finger, signaling, Can it, Barbie. He opens his eyes to mine and with a strained, almost tortured voice, says, "I love you." To our much-astounded stares, he inches up enough to level our eyes, snakes his hand around my neck and pulls me to his lips. And as if the last few minutes never happened, he releases me and plunges himself onto the empty chair next to us. We follow his every questionable move closely. He snatches a piece of pita bread from the little basket on the table and plops it into his mouth. His lips pull up as he chews on the bread. "I'm damn good, aren't I? You totally bought it."

"You got me. I was about to call Daniel and tell him I found me a real man," I say flatly.

"One of the scenes from *Urban Heartbreak*. Fucking cheesy, ah?"

"Could have skipped the lip lock there, movie star," I say. Ian grins in response.

"I actually love it," Tasha says dreamingly. "Can't wait to watch it."

Ian grins at Tasha, blows her a kiss, and grabs one of the menus. "So what's good in this joint?"

We've all polished nearly half of our dishes and had a tasting orgy, trying each other's food, when Tasha takes a sip of her lemonade and says, "I got an offer for a relocation."

My head jolts up. I blurt, "You're leaving Stark Software?"

She shakes her head. Ian drops the last piece of pita bread and hummus into his mouth and cleans his lips with a napkin, his full attention on Tasha. Tasha's stare runs from Ian to me and back. "Actually, Daniel offered to let me manage the Thai office setup." Her eyes stay on mine. "And I'm going to accept his offer. That's my important meeting," she adds, biting on her bottom lip.

Ian and I trade confused stares. "You'll be moving to Asia?" I ask, too muddled to form a more intelligent question. *What in the hell?*

Her wicked grin turns up on her lips. "That's right, sweetie, Thailand is indeed in Asia. You really know your geography. I'm proud." She pats my hand.

I don't even have it in me to come up with a proper retaliation.

"For how long?" Ian asks, the most solemn I've heard him in, well, a very long time.

"Not sure yet. I'll supervise the setup, which I believe should take a good few months, and then we'll see. There's an option to stay there and co-run it with a local site manager after he or she is hired. But I'll have to go through the hiring process just like any other candidate."

"He didn't tell me anything about it," I say under my breath.

"Hales, there's wasn't anything to tell before my decision," Tasha says.

"Why didn't *you* tell us?" Ian asks, seeming no less perturbed than I am.

At least, she has the decency to look somewhat repentant. "Guys, see, um, you need to understand, I wanted to make the decision by myself. I didn't want anyone influencing it. It's a huge thing for me, and for once, I wanted to rely on my judgment alone."

"Did we ever force you to do anything you didn't want to do, Tash?" Ian asks mildly disappointed.

Her eyes downcast, she forks the remainder of her dish but

never actually brings it up to her mouth. "Rafa said you guys would be upset."

"Just hold the fuck up," Ian snaps. In unison, we both shift our stares his way. "Rafael knew about it and Hales and I didn't? That's such a dick move."

"He's coming along with me," she breathes in response.

My eyes grow in tandem to Ian's headshake. I take a deep breath. "Why don't we all just calm down for a moment? Now Tasha, spill it all out, *everything." Before we make you douse your torch and leave Friends Island.*

Half an hour later with our lunchtime breaks dwindled down to mere minutes, both Ian and I are somewhat placated. As much as one can be with such news. In good old Natasha Taylor fashion, Tasha has done a skillful job at clarifying her motives while stroking and cajoling her soul mates' wounded egos into loving her again.

"That's so fucked up! Hales, you are going to start popping out little Starky humans, and Tash is going to reign a group of little almond-shaped humans," Ian says, riled up, dropping a couple of notes on the table. "What's happening to us?"

I rub his bicep fondly. "We're growing up, I guess."

"You might want to give it a try, too." Tasha grins at him.

"Never." Ian pouts.

"Hey guys, how about a sleepover tomorrow? Daniel is traveling again; keep me company y'all."

"PJ party, I'm in," Tasha says, draping her purse over her shoulder.

"Growing up, my impeccable ass," Ian snorts. "I'm bringing da liquids." He winks, kisses our cheeks, and strides away with a hard to miss swagger that claims a few turned heads in his wake.

Chapter 18: Powerfully. Fiercely. Complete.

"Hey, baby." I turn from the sketchpad on my lap to give Daniel a semi-hostile look.

"What's up?" He takes a couple of steps my way, where I'm working on a drawing, nestled on the living room sofa.

I raise my hand his way, gesturing for him to stop. "Thank you for sending my friend to another country and failing to mention it." I narrow my glare. "Unless you have one helluva excuse or an incredibly rare diamond on you, I would warmly recommend you stay back."

Daniel's eyes light up in amusement which immediately dissipates my feigned anger. He makes a whole production of patting his pockets with one hand. He shakes his head, his mouth slightly twisted. "Sorry, no diamond." A hint of a smile plays at the corner of his lips as he brings forward a pizza box. "Tony's pizza instead?"

"Even better." I set my sketchpad aside on its face, trying to hide my own smile.

"Ever heard of the saying 'Beware of Greeks Bearing Gifts'?" He shrugs off his blazer and drops it on the sofa next to me.

"Oh, you trying to penetrate my gate is nothing I should be too cautious about, on the contrary . . ." I beam at him, only to be gifted with a wicked, sweetly wicked, smile.

I watch Daniel as he kicks off his shoes and lowers to sit on the coffee table in front of me. I keep my eyes on him, more than enjoying his looks in a casual black tee and jeans. His hair is a bit longer than usual; a couple of lighter clusters of gold fall and cover his eyebrow as he turns to me with a slice of heavenly smelling pepperoni pizza. Melted cheese strings swing from either side. I take the offering and bring it to my mouth, closing my eyes, savoring the perfect taste. Daniel watches me, taking a bite of his own slice.

I lick the salty, delectable grease off my lips. "I thought we told each other everything." I raise my eyes, challenging his.

Daniel takes another bite of his slice and swallows it down. "This doesn't concern *us*. It's about an offer I gave one of my employees." I roll my eyes, a gesture he bluntly disregards. "It's a good opportunity for her. You should be happy for her. She made a wise decision."

"Of course, I'm glad for her. I'll miss her, that's all. A lot."

"There are planes."

Simple. Daniel Stark simple.

"But isn't Thailand dangerous?" I ask; Daniel's hostage experience there just a few months ago is still a fresh and taunting memory.

"It was a period of political instability. The situation has calmed down now. Bangkok is quite safe. Obviously, we'll make sure the employees take the appropriate precautions. We're in close contact with the embassy, and we're strictly following the government's travel advisories for the city." He places his hand on my knee. "Hales, rest assured I'm never going to put any of my employees in danger. Now, can we stop discussing Natasha's career and maybe talk about yours?"

Where did this come from? "What about mine?"

Daniel tips his chin toward the side table. "What were you working on?"

I lick pizza off my fingers under Daniel's more than engrossed stare. Giving my middle finger some good old-fashioned suction for good measure. Daniel's irises darken at my little show. I smirk and reach for the sketchpad, flipping back some pages to hide what I was really working on. He takes the sketchpad and studies the drawing. A modern interpretation of Snow White in which Miss White is a badass president of an outlaw motorcycle club with the dwarfs as her entourage.

"It's great."

"And you're biased."

Daniel twists his mouth, drops the sketchpad onto his lap, and turns to gaze at me. Hazel eyes wordlessly scolding. "Hales, it's fucking brilliant. And it's about time you did something about it instead of wasting your time on a job you don't really need."

I fold my arms across my chest in defense. "I like my job."

"More than illustrating?" Scarred eyebrow arches at me.

I shake my head.

"Wouldn't you like to do this for a living instead?"

I bob my head.

"Then you should pitch your work with some agents."

"I'll think about it."

"We both know you won't. You'll just keep hiding your work in a drawer. You're good, Hales. Start believing in yourself." He watches me closely. "Tell you what, anything you want if you start looking for an agent."

"Anything?" I ask, holding his gaze firmly.

He folds his own arms across his wide chest. "Anything."

I rise to my feet, set the sketchpad aside, and bend to sit on his lap. With tender kisses and gentle strokes of bristled cheeks, I soothe him for the blow. "Talk to someone about what you went through in Thailand and I'll pitch to every possible agent on the planet."

He watches me with hard eyes for some strained beats. His jaw ticking. "Deal."

I let out a relieved breath, looking at him in wonder. *Really*?

A little wrinkle sets above his nose. "Why do you look so surprised?"

I lick my lip, trying to find the right words. "It's that important to you, that you'd be willing to actually . . ." I don't get to finish my sentence.

He shakes his head, his lips in a grim smile. "I'm actually surprised that by now you still can't comprehend just how important you are to me. *You* always come first. Just as I'm doing what I want to do, and enjoy it, I want the same for you. It's very simple, Hales. I want you happy." Mischief infiltrates his serious expression. "Happy and naked." He squeezes my butt.

· · ·

Brushing my teeth, I shift my eyes to look at Daniel through the vanity mirror. He pulls his shirt up over his head and throws it into the hamper. He rinses his toothbrush. Reaching for the toothpaste, his eyes meet mine in the mirror. I return his smile with a mouth full of suds and toothbrush. Aimlessly, my mind wanders to the night Daniel told me he wanted me for the first time, at the Stark Software fundraiser. It feels like a lifetime ago. The smile on my face is not something I'm controlling anymore.

Daniel halts his brushing. "Hey, what are you smiling like that for?"

My smile expands. Holding my stare over the mirror, his own crooked smile broadens as he moves to stand behind me. One of his hands goes back to brushing while the other settles on my hip. I tilt forward to rinse my mouth, deliberately brushing my butt against his groin. As I straighten up, his hand on my hip pulls me back, closer to his chest.

"I was just remembering that morning when you came all the way to YOU just 'cause you had to kiss me."

His lips stretch into a grin around the toothbrush. He lowers down from behind me to reach the sink. He rinses his mouth, and I take the chance to press a kiss on his muscled shoulder. Returning to stand behind me, he sends his hand to my waist and turns me to face him. His hands move to my hip and lift me to perch on the vanity. He pushes my legs apart, settling between them.

He leans in to kiss my lips lightly. "Nothing has changed. I still feel exactly the same." He kisses me again, this time with greater intensity.

"Same here," I say as we draw back. Reaching for the night lotion, I open the little jar. "You ruined me for anyone else that morning. No, wait; it was actually the night before, at that fundraiser."

Daniel takes the lotion from my hand, sinks the tip of his finger in the pinkish cream, and sets it aside. He gives me a soft smile, dabbing four little spots on my face. Forehead, cheeks, and ends with my chin. He presses a kiss to my nose and starts smoothing the lotion onto my skin. I wrap my legs around his pelvis, tipping my face back, fluttering my eyes closed. The gentle touch of his fingers on my skin feels wonderful.

"You ruined me for others when you stepped into my kitchen."

I open my eyes, which are lightly heated by his proximity. "Oh wait, it was actually that graceful 'fuck me.'" His lopsided smile makes an appearance.

I return his bright stare from under my lashes. My eyes descend to his lips, to his carved chest, to the sprinkle of darker hair leading into his jeans. I slowly trail my eyes back to his and huskily whisper, "Fuck me."

Daniel's stare dims as he leans in to meet my lips with a kiss that revs up the heat dominating each part of me since he moved to stand behind me. Our tongues graze, taste, smooth against one another, accelerating the rhythm to aggressive, possessive, and needy. He breaks the almost manic connection, his eyes searing into mine. Taking a step back, he rips my shorts off me, sliding them down my legs. His fingers find the hem of my panties and ever so slowly drag them down my body. Determined, he continues to free me of my tank top. Still watching me like he's about to drag me into his lair, he unbuttons his jeans. Pushing them down together with his boxers, his hands slide to my inner thighs, spreading them further apart. He watches me for a heated beat as I'm splayed open before him, my breathing heavier. My eyes hooded, my lips parted, my inside humming and begging for his touch. His hand moves to hold himself at the base, the other slowly stroking upward. A pant leaves my lips, watching him, every piece of my skin heats up. Hazel stare drinks me in as one of his hands grabs my hip while the other guides him to me. He teases, rubbing himself at my heated spot, repeatedly stealing incoherent, raw sounds out of me. I fall back to rest on my elbows for a better view of the sensual display. He stiffens, his breath held as he sinks into me. In unison, we let out an expel of pleasure. And then, as I asked, he fucks me. Powerfully. Fiercely. Complete with untamed craze.

Chapter 19: Sweets, Booze, and a Colonic

I resurface from a deep sleep to gentle strokes of my hair. Blinking a couple of times, I work to adjust my vision to the faintly illuminated room. I crane my neck to look up at Daniel, who meets my gaze with a gentle, lopsided smile. He sits next to me on the bed in a suit, his freshly showered scent bathing me.

"What's the time?" I say in a raspy voice.

"Two a.m." He dips his mouth to press a kiss on my forehead. I study him under the soft light coming from the slightly ajar bathroom door in the otherwise dark room. He brings his hand to brush a wayward curl from my face. "I'm leaving in five. There's something I wanted to tell you before I go."

"What is it?"

He takes my hand, lacing his fingers with mine. "The results came in," he says. I wait for him to go on, unable to breathe. "It's not mine."

I close my eyes, pushing out the breath I've been holding. I squeeze his hand, my eyes caressing his handsome features. "I love you."

He slowly leans in to press another kiss on my forehead. Lowering his lips, he kisses the tip of my nose and moves on to my lips. He brushes my lips with a series of gentle kisses. His mouth trails lower, leaving supple kisses over my neck. Reaching my collarbone, his lips kiss a path from one side to the other.

I watch him as he straightens to sit. His fingers thread at either side of my temple, tender eyes on mine. His low voice breaks the silence. "Love is a weak word to express how I feel about you, Hales."

I rise up to sit, wrap my arms around his neck, and kiss him so hard, I drop him back to the bed. I kiss him some more, finding it almost impossible to finally let him go.

. . .

"What do you say?" Tasha asks. Tilting her head sideways, she examines what Ian and I are studying with great concentration. Seeming undecided, she says, "Maybe we should drink first. Alcohol is known to free your imagination and fuel creativity." The three of us exchange animated stares. "Okay, drink up," she commands.

In unison, Tasha and Ian take the shot glass before them and throw it back as if it's their job. A wince moves in succession from Tasha to Ian.

"Shit's lethal," Ian murmurs, heaving a breath.

"l'chaim. . ." I mumble to my sparkling water.

A sinister grin rises up Tasha's lips. "Suck it up, big boy." She pats Ian's shoulder. "It'll grow hair on your chest." She shrugs off his middle finger gesture with light laughter and turns to the counter. Ian and I mirror her as she resumes studying our production.

"Feels like something is missing." Ian's words trail off pensively. He circles his finger in the air, pointing at the object we're studying. "Maybe more lubricant?"

I can't help the humored snort from escaping my mouth.

"What?" he says with a chuckle. "It'll slide better into your mouth." Tasha bursts into a giggle at his side.

"I actually love me some old-fashioned friction, if ya know what I mean." I wink at him to be rewarded with an impish chuckle.

"How about we pour some warm chocolate on it? What do you say?" Tasha asks, her lips stretched mischievously.

Ian and I give each other an assessing glance. "It might soften it, but I prefer it hard," he says, hamming it up with the gravity in his voice.

"More whipped cream?" I try.

On cue, Tasha snatches the Reddi Wip, sprays out a foamy string, and sends out the tip of her tongue for a taste. "Yeah, definitely."

"Tash, Tash, Tash." Ian shakes his head. "What's up with the late-night soft porn? You trying to make my boy parts tingle?"

Tasha claps a hand to her mouth. "Ohmygod, you're on to me." She blinks a couple of times. "Maybe it's time I confessed." She captures Ian's stare. "My secret lifelong dream, mysterious even to me, has been to convert you." She gestures her hand over Ian; adding a sultry hue to her voice, she says, "All of this hotness unattainable, yet so close."

"Can't blame ya," Ian says with a light sway of his head. He gives our creation one last glance before declaring, *"Perfect.* Ladies?" His smile grows sinister. "Ready for some oral play?"

Marilyn's "Happy Birthday, Mr. President" has nothing on my voice when I say, "I thought you'd never ask."

We settle down on the rug. Ian is wedged between Tash and me with the obscene bowl of banana split we've concocted on his lap.

"I swear this is the most hazardous dish on the planet," I say, digging a spoon into the summit of sugar, fat, and God knows how much artificial goodness.

Tasha brings a spoonful to her lips. "We should've booked a bypass for later, just in case."

"Or at least, a colonic," I add.

Ian snorts. "Okay, shut your faces now, or I'll banish you to the kitchen. This is the best part."

Ian, Tasha, and I, spoons held in mouths, grow silent and stare at the wide screen. For a long, focused beat, we're all fixated on the screen. We sigh in unison when the scene of Ryan Gosling hot and heavy with, who really cares, fades to black.

"Now, this is the stuff dreams are made of," Ian says, pausing the movie on an almost full frontal. Naturally, we nod in agreement. "So, Hales, are you knocked up yet?"

Come again? Startled, my head jerks Ian's way. "Wha?"

He twists his mouth. "Do you have a little Starky human in your womb, yet?" then, "Un Starky bebé en tu útero?"

"How do you even know how to say uterus in Spanish?" Tasha wonders out loud.

"The real question should be how did we get from that." I throw my hand to the screen. "To whether I'm with a child."

Ian grins. "Ryan always makes my ovaries rattle. And ovaries, you know . . ." His smile morphs into a smirk.

Tasha studies me for a lengthened moment with narrowed eyes and a start of a smile.

"What?" I ask.

"Well, are you?"

"Don't you guys have any boundaries?"

Their mocking snorts come in stereo and so does the adamant, "*No.*"

I take a deep breath. "I might be," comes out on an exhale.

Ian's features turn confused in tandem to the crease of Tasha's brows. "What does that mean?" Tasha is the one to voice the question.

A mini-debate starts in my head before I decide to spill it. They are Tasha and Ian, after all. The only people with a standing front-row seat to my crazy. "Um, I'm a couple of days late, but it doesn't really mean anything. And I bought, like, a bazillion and one home pregnancy tests. I kid you not. But I can't bring myself to actually take one." They both look at me with patience, letting me get it all out. "But, on the other hand, I don't even want to know. I'm freaked out and excited at the same time. Do I even make any sense?" I don't let them answer. "I really try not to obsess about it. Because eventually, I'll find out whether I want to or not." I end my meltdown with shoving a spoonful of ice cream into my mouth.

"You'll eventually know? Like, when a little hand pops out of your vagina and waves?" Ian waves a little wave, backing his question.

Tasha rolls her eyes with a thin smile and turns to me. "Don't you want to find out?"

"Yes and no." I sigh. *Yes, you're a nutjob. Great maternal material here. But look at the bright side, these two are used to it. And can easily give you a run for your money. The boy especially.*

"Let's all take one together." I can't help breaking into laughter. Yes, that came from Ian. *I rest my case!*

"Moron." Tasha shakes her head, her lips in a wide grin.

"What?" Ian chuckles. "I'm serious. Come on, it'll be a hoot."

I shake my head five minutes later as we're all leaning against the bathroom wall, waiting for our results. *Well, if you can't beat them, join the not of sound mind.* Even though I'm freaked to my bones, I can't stop snickering, watching Ian wait for his results.

"Great! I get to cross this off my bucket list tonight," Ian says, yanking me out of my stress bubble.

Tasha and I crane our heads that are rested on the wall, squinting our eyes to look at him.

"You had taking a pregnancy test on your bucket list?" Tasha gives Ian an incredulous stare.

He smirks at her. I choose to believe he's messing with us. *There's just so much lunacy one can encompass.*

Tasha checks her watch. "Ready, Hales?"

I nod.

We scatter to three different corners of the ample bathroom. We made sure to place each stick in a concealed spot. Tight as we are, there are some things one should never be exposed to.

"Thank God, negative," Ian declares in Ian fashion.

"Can you please stop waving your stick at us? There was a purpose to keeping it covered," Tasha chides.

"Oh honey, don't insult me. A stick?" Ian drops his eyes to his sweats-clad groin, tilting his head from side to side. "Um, I'd go with a trunk."

Tasha and I throw our eyes to the ceiling.

"Negative," Tasha says, wrapping her stick in toilet paper. She shifts her eyes to me, mirroring Ian.

"Negative." The mixed emotions in me are jarring.

They both come closer, placing their arms around either side of my waist. "You okay?" Tasha asks.

"I guess." I shrug, having a hard time wrapping my head around what I'm feeling. How can one feel such great relief and immense disappointment at the same time?

"Look at the positive side. We can now drop sweet and move on back to booze." Ian squeezes me into him.

"I'll pass on the alcohol, thank you," I say, discarding my stick.

"Great! More for us," Tasha sings.

For the next couple of hours, I'm not able to think about the results even once, for I'm too occupied trying not to lose a lung due to excessive laughter. The combination of my friends and booze is practically fatal.

"Awake?" Ian says to the calm silence, his voice uncharacteristically grave. Too exhausted and comfortable, we've decided to camp out in the wilderness of the living room.

Tasha and I raise our heads from either side of his chest. "Yesss?" Tasha questions.

I'm not sure what makes my heart drop; the tone of his voice or what actually comes out of his mouth when he says, "I ended things with Josh."

"Oh, Ian," Tasha says.

"Are you okay?" I whisper, finding Tasha's eyes through the dark. We exchange a concerned stare. "You sure it was the right thing to do?" My voice has the same gentle quality as Tasha.

I feel the rolling shake in his chest before his chuckle reaches us. "Told you I'm a terrific actor," he says over his rolling laughter. The laughter elevates when two thrown pillows meet his face at the same time.

"Idiot," Tasha murmurs.

When his chuckles subside, and Tasha and I are back to snuggling on his chest, Ian says, "We didn't break up, but we're moving in together."

Needless to say, not much sleep occurs after this bomb.

Chapter 20: Because Sometimes
You Just Have to

"Hayley? What *are you* doing here so early?"

"I can ask you the same thing, Boss." I stifle a yawn, swiveling in my chair to face Josh.

"I have an early budget meeting I need to prepare for. What's your excuse?"

"I don't sleep very well alone." I leave out the part that each time Daniel is either about to board a plane or land, I stress out. Let's just say, I was able to breathe a little better once I got a text, about half an hour ago, telling me he's back on SF soil.

Josh's smile climbs up to his lips. The same one that seems to come as a reflex each time Daniel is mentioned. Before my declaration turns into a gabfest, I ask, "I'm going to get coffee, get you anything?" In my defense, I haven't had my first cup of coffee yet, making any minor action, let alone conversing, too much to accomplish.

"God, please. Caramel Macchiato. Oh, and a cinnamon roll." This time, The Smile holds a grateful glee.

I nod and turn on my heel. Deep in thought, I make it to

reception. Everything from missing Daniel, to Thing One and Thing Two's sleepover the other night and the test results, to the cute cowgirl boots I ordered online, distract me from realizing the reception area is not actually as abandoned as it appears to be. Our heavily pierced, impudent of a brat receptionist might have not arrived yet, but apparently there *is* someone in the room. The movement in my peripheral view and the weight of a stare on me makes me still.

Looking up, realizing who it is, I do a double take. No one can make my heart go as wild as it beats right now nor pull off sexy-disheveled like Daniel does. With overgrown stubble, unruly hair, and a white, slightly wrinkled, untucked shirt, he couldn't look more decadent.

"What are you doing here?" flies out of my mouth.

Daniel pushes himself off the wall and strides my way. Crooked smile present. His arms wrap around my waist, pulling me to him. His lips descend to hover over mine. "I didn't want to start my morning without kissing you." It's pretty obvious he came here directly from the airport. A notion that adds a sprinkle of ecstasy to my overall hard swooning.

When he tries to ease back, I secure my hand around his neck, making it impossible. I attack his mouth, releasing all the pent-up longing from not seeing him for a few days. He chuckles into my kiss, but his tongue quickly joins the tempo my unleashed one is dictating. Reluctantly, after some wonderful moments, I ease off. Not only for the sake of being in a public place but with said public place also happening to be my place of work.

"I missed you," I say, lacing my fingers with his.

"I can see that." He rewards me with one of his extra sinful grins. Tugging on my hand, he brings me closer to his side. "Missed you, too." He plants a kiss on the crown of my head.

"I was just going to get coffee." I tip my chin toward the door. "I'll walk you there."

On our way to get coffee, we tell each other about the days we spent apart. Among other less important things, I tell him about taking a pregnancy test, leaving out the part where Ian and Tash took one with me. His reaction couldn't make me less edgy and at the same time love him more.

He kisses my temple. "There's a next time." Something about the confidence and coolness Daniel emits makes *me* self-assured, worriless, and . . . blissful. Because no matter what, whatever happens, when he is by my side, everything is just . . . better.

Fifteen minutes later, Daniel kisses me good-bye like it's his job and takes off in the Veyron. The last look he gives me tells me just how the next time we're alone will play. A look that buzzes inside me. Two paper cups and a cinnamon roll in hand, and pulsing lips, I make my way back to the office. I'd be boldly lying if I said that I'm not mentally envisioning Daniel throwing me on a bed and devouring me as I hand Josh his order, flushed, mind you.

My phone pings with an incoming message, distracting Josh and me from the money-beverage exchange. "I'm just . . ." I start to say, and Josh nods, only interested in ravenously eyeing his coffee.

Daniel: H, want to play hooky with me?
I text back.
And do what?
Daniel: Me.
Have mercy on my ovaries, D. It's as if he can read my deepest and filthiest thoughts. The earlier pulsing I felt on my lips now runs amuck to every part of me. I swallow hard and look up at Josh.

"You okay, Hayley? You're a bit flushed." Josh's features harden with concern. He clutches his hand around my shoulder. "Are you having trouble breathing? Maybe you should sit down."

Hell, that's where I'm going. "Umm, I think I might be coming down with something." *A stark case of D-bola, Boss.* "Um, would it be okay if I work from home today?" The little devil with the red corset that's perched on my shoulder gives me a thumbs-up.

"Oh, don't worry about work. Just get some rest. We'll be fine. Do you want me to drive you home?"

I shake my head, feeling even worse for lying now, what with the genuine concern Josh is showing. However, said feeling vanishes once I shoot Daniel a response. After all, one should get her daily dose of vitamin D.

Race you home!

Almost instantly, Daniel's name flickers across my screen. "Hey," I answer through a grin.

"Drive safely." His voice doesn't hold even an ounce of humor. My eyes fly to the skies right after he hangs up.

A message lands in my cell as I'm about to start the car. With the key in the ignition, foot still on the brake, I check it out.

Daniel: HAYLEY, DRIVE SAFELY!

I shake my head and toss the phone into the passenger seat. *Overbearing psycho.*

. . .

I press the remote, waiting for the garage door to rise. My smile blossoms at the sight of Daniel leaning on the Veyron, his legs stretched before him, crossed at the ankles, waiting.

Out of the corner of my eye, I see him rolling up his sleeves as I rear park next to him. I push the button to close the garage door, drape my bag over my shoulder, and climb out. Daniel prowls my way, getting there before I'm even able to shut the car's door. With eyes drinking me hungrily, he sends his hand to my strap on my shoulder. He slides it down and unceremoniously throws my handbag into the driver's seat. Wordlessly, he takes my hand and walks me to the front of my car. I watch him with hooded eyes as he leans in to kiss me. Gradually, he presses me back till my rear meets the warm hood of the car. His hands that were holding my cheeks, slowly trace down my neck, collarbone, breasts and waist, till they reach the hem of my shirtdress. I let out a quiet whimper, deepening our kiss. Our teeth collide when the kiss gains momentum. Daniel's fingers graze my skin, pulling my dress up my thighs. Never leaving his mouth, I send my hand to his slacks. When I slide my hand inside his boxers, a raw growl rumbles from his chest. Abruptly, he grabs my hips and lifts me up. I land with a light jerk on the still cooling hood. Daniel's eyes are two pools of heat as he gazes at me, yanking his belt off, unbuttoning his pants, and letting them drop to his ankles.

"Spread your legs for me, Hales," comes a gruff command.

Staring back at him with no less desire and biting on my bottom lip, I slowly do as asked. Daniel takes a step forward, settling between my parted thighs. Never breaking our heated stare, he sends his hand to my panties. I let out a breathy sigh when he slides his thumb under the fabric. His hazel stare becomes scorching as he pushes his thumb into me. I close my eyes, relishing the current of pleasure.

"Hales," the command in his voice makes me open my eyes back into his. Doing what he wordlessly asked of me, I keep my stare on him as he grazes over my heated skin. His thumb works me, putting the right amount of pressure to elicit shudders up my thighs.

With his free hand, he takes mine. He threads his fingers through mine and guides me to wrap around his shaft. We watch each other with wild eyes as his thumb keeps circling me, and our hands glide together over his length. Daniel lifts our joined hands, bringing them near his mouth. He presses a warm kiss to my skin and moves my hand to hold his waist. He sends his arm to my lower back and slides me slightly forward.

Not breaking eye contact, as he pushes my panties aside with one hand and brings himself to me with the other. We both let out a guttural pant as he buries himself in me. Steadily, he slams into me and pulls backs. A light sheen covers his upper lip, the frown between his brows deepening as his thrusts become fiercer, deeper, sending me climbing higher and higher.

"Daniel," comes out on a needy exhale.

"Yes, baby, that's it."

His hand slides between us, and when it reaches my pulsing peak, I cry out incoherently. I start to spasm around him with an electrical current tidal in my core, sending me to lose myself in the incredible feeling of release, at the moment, in Daniel.

• • •

I blink one eye open, checking my phone. *God, I've napped for over four hours.* After I freshen up in the bathroom, I make my way to get coffee, knotting my hair in a bun. Tipping my eyes up as I step into the kitchen space, I stop short.

"Good morning, baby." Daniel grins at me, handing a ladle to the cute blonde fussing around beside him. *Handing a ladle to the cute blonde beside him?!*

"Hi?" Not sure if that actually came out of my mouth, as I'm too busy studying the domestic scene taking place before me. A cropped-haired blonde with huge green eyes and a nose ring takes the ladle from Daniel while smiling at me.

Daniel's smile turns into a full-blown smirk as his eyes lazily take me in, reminding me that the only clothing I'm currently donning is a shocking pink bra and matching thong. I lightly smile at the appreciative glee in his stare.

"Hey, Hayley." Blondie with the apron waves my way. I give the scene in front of me another gauging glance. There are several bowls with fresh vegetables, grains, and tofu piled up on the kitchen island. Daniel stands beside Ms. Apron in a pair of jeans and a snug white tee, barefoot and beaming.

I twist my mouth, not exactly the greatest fan of the fact that another woman gets to see his bare feet. Okay, that sounded borderline wacko, even in my head. Well, I don't like it. Big. Deal. Moving on . . .

My possessiveness cracks her knuckles, stretching her neck from side to side. Yes, it's she, and she's a badass. Though internally I flinch at my scanty appearance, I hold my head up and saunter toward the island.

I wrap my right arm around Daniel's waist, and casually send my left hand to the pistachio bowl on the counter. I plop one of the nuts into my mouth. "Having fun playing with *my* ladle?" I say to no one in particular; my eyes, though, are hard on the lady holding the incriminating utensil.

They both chuckle in unison. *How cute. Not.*

"She's exactly how you described her," she tells Daniel. "I'm Nadine." Her smile trails to me. "Daniel has probably told you about me. I'm going to be your personal chef."

I turn to look at Daniel in query.

Daniel kisses my temple. "Thought it would be useful to learn how to cook healthier food."

"What is it? A surprise 'why don't we hone your cooking skills a little' party?" I narrow my eyes, my lips slightly quirked.

"Though your cooking skills could use a little honing. . ."

Daniel's eyes dance. I slap his chest with pistachio salt sprinkled fingers. "It's for the both of us." And as if we don't have an audience, Daniel's hand moves to rest on my bare stomach. "Told you, I want to make sure you eat healthier food." Warmness floods my belly where his hand rests.

Nadine, whipping eggs, is all easy smiles.

"Would have been nice to get a little heads-up about having someone over. I'm at a bit of a disadvantage here." I whisper, and in a louder voice, I add, "I'm going to change into something *less* comfortable." *Like actual clothes.*

Daniel's eyes zoom in on my breasts while his hand moves to my bare rear. "Don't mind me."

"Or me," Nadine adds, her lips tipped up.

I let out a finesse-full snort. "You," I press my finger into Daniel's chest, "can make me coffee, Mr. hire a personal chef without telling me." His response? Squeezing my bum and planting a kiss on my forehead.

"How do you take your coffee? Why don't you let me pamper you?" Nadine asks, chopping fat stalks of asparagus.

"Um," I start, slowly walking backward out of the kitchen. It's safe to say Nadine has seen enough of my butt to last her a lifetime.

"Double shot, extra hot, cappuccino, and go easy on the froth," Daniel says, peeling a cucumber.

"Got it," Nadine says.

"Thanks, Nadine. . ." I say over my shoulder and scurry to get dressed.

. . .

"I swear, if I weren't already engaged, I'd propose to you," I tell Nadine, polishing off yet another spoonful of Korean fried cauliflower that ends with a moan. The lady gives good vegan.

Daniel gives me an admonishing look. I wink at him with a cheeky smile.

Nadine smiles into her wineglass. "Well, thank you for inviting me to stay. It was an absolute pleasure, but I should get going." She starts gathering her stuff.

Somewhere between Daniel getting bored of kitchen labor and a burned, over reduced soy sauce courtesy of me, Daniel came to the conclusion that the whole us cooking healthy wouldn't work, so he hired Nadine to cook for us three times a week. Right after, we invited her to join us for the delicious meal she ended up cooking all by herself. In my defense, all through the cooking process, I dedicatedly helped with tasting.

I show Nadine to the door, once again declaring my insta-love to her and her culinary abilities. "Oh Hayley, I'd have definitely said yes if you would have actually proposed." She grins at me, closing the door behind her.

Smiling, I make my way back to the kitchen where Daniel is resting his hip on the island, checking his phone.

"Nadine could totally take Ian and Tasha's place when they are gone," I say, loading the fridge with the food Nadine prepared for us.

"Ouch." Daniel chuckles. "That's vicious, baby. They haven't left yet, and you're already shortlisting?" He lifts his eyes from his cell.

I smile, though the thought of Tasha leaving for Thailand and Ian for a shooting in freaking Milwaukee sits heavily on my heart. "Hey, the woman *can cook*." I close the fridge and turn to face him.

Daniel smiles lightly. "I'm glad I'm not being replaced yet." He tosses his phone on the counter, his attention on me.

I wrap my arms around his neck, my face tilted up. "No one can ever give me what you give me."

"And what would that be?" A crooked smile awaits my response.

I kiss his jaw. "You." I lean back to look at him. "Thank you for everything you're doing for me."

"Thank you for everything you are." He inclines to press a light kiss to my lips.

"Daniel Stark, are you turning into a hopeless romantic in your old age?"

Daniel reaches for his beer bottle on the island beside us. He takes a long drink, his face tilted sideways. "Just trying to get into your panties again," he says to the bottle's mouth with a grin.

I fabricate a pout. "You just killed a perfectly cheesy moment."

He places the bottle back and pulls me closer to him. His hands grip my hips, and he lifts me up to straddle him. Instinctively, I lock my legs around him.

"Um, wha –"

His mouth meshes with mine, silencing my question.

"I've been waiting to do this since you marched into the kitchen earlier half naked," Daniel says to my neck, walking us to the bedroom.

Chapter 21: Something in the Water?

"Psst . . . I'll show you mine if you show me yours."

I swivel around in my chair to the creepy whisper. Reflexively, my face lights up to Ian's smile.

"What of mine could *you* possibly want to see?"

Ian's smile turns from cheery to sleazy in a nanosecond. "The naked pics of your man on your phone."

I shake my head. "Sorry to disappoint. No such thing exists."

"It's a shame. Start taking them tonight. Tell you what. I can do you a favor and give you some pointers." He tucks his hands into his pockets in nonchalance.

"Bet you would." I give him a quick once-over. Ian in an all-black ensemble is a sight to enjoy.

"No seriously, gorgeous. I'm talking scientifically proven material here. The significance of a relationship is measured by how much of your phone storage is utilized by your spouse's nudity."

I turn to save the document I was working on before Ian interrupted me with the interpersonal relationship scientific breakthrough.

"Let me show you this artistic collection of Josh." I hear his steps coming closer.

"No!" I yelp, squeezing my eyes shut. "Ian, I swear!"

He snickers beside me. "C'mon, we're lunching together. Let's go get Josh."

With my eyes still shut in horror, I say, "Just put the phone down, and everything will be all right. Put the phone down, Ian."

Ian grabs my hands and pulls me out of my chair. "It's in my pocket." I finally open my eyes. "Anyhow, you wouldn't be able to handle it."

"What wouldn't she be able to handle," Josh asks, joining us.

"Oh, believe me, you don't want to know," I say.

Familiar with the cuckoo nest that's his boyfriend's mind, Josh lets it go.

"So where do you want to go?" I ask, quickly changing the subject.

. . .

"How about we order several starters to share?" Josh asks after we all examine the rich menus for too long, still undecided.

"Good idea," I say, and Ian nods.

While Josh places our order with the bulky, energetic waitress, Ian tells me new details about the movie. A small twinge tugs at my heart when he says that they finally have a date to start shooting.

"For how long will you be staying there?" I ask, bringing a piece of bread to my mouth.

"Obviously, it's subject to change, depending on how it goes, budget, and shit, but they are talking about four to six weeks."

"So you're leaving just a couple of days before Tash, uh?" I sigh. "Everybody is leaving me."

Ian nods and turns to give Josh an inscrutable glance. They seem to have some sort of wordless conversation. I study Josh's frown lines. Or maybe it's an argument.

Josh clears his throat. "About that, Hayley." He smiles at me, but this time, his smile has a timid air to it, maybe even an apologetic one. Ian's eyes squint my way. "I know I'm not as important as Ian and Natasha, but I'm sort of leaving too."

"What do you mean?" I ask Josh, but it's Ian's expression I'm trying to decode.

"I'm leaving YOU. I gave my notice last week."

"Wow," is all I manage to say through the questions running in my head. "When is your last day?"

"The end of next month. I've decided to take a couple of weeks off and join Ian on set before starting at the new place." Not a bad idea when it comes to Ian and his wayward mind. I wouldn't test the proverb "absence makes the heart grow fonder" on Ian. Not for the time being, at least.

Ian smiles at Josh.

I take a sip of my drink. "Where are you starting, if you don't mind me asking?"

Josh shakes his head. "I haven't told anyone yet, but I trust you to keep it under wraps for a while."

I nod.

"I'm going to be the managing editor of *Gentleman*. I'm done dealing with ladies issues." His trademark smile shines at me.

"I understand. That's great. I'm so glad for you."

"Would you be interested in joining me there?" He forks a fried calamari.

I look up at him, chewing on the vegetarian tikka masala in my mouth. I swallow, my mind processing the question. "Thanks for the offer, but I think I'm good where I am. It won't be the same without you there, though."

We trade amicable smiles.

"So yeah, he's going to be chaperoning me instead of tyrannizing you," Ian says, flinging back a couple of stray strands from his forehead.

"A. I won't have too much time to keep you company with settling into our new home." Josh wipes his mouth with a napkin. "B. I think I can say it was actually Hayley who was tyrannizing me."

"That I can believe." Ian smirks at me.

"Not letting you drag me into this," I say and turn to Josh. "If there's anything I can help with, packing/unpacking or whatever, don't hesitate to ask."

"Sure. Appreciate it."

"Anyhow, nothing much for me to do these days. I'm going to be left all alone. Is there something in the water around here? Everyone seems to be leaving." I end with a sigh.

It's an almost impossible task to get back to work after lunch. I hug the coffee mug with both hands, aimlessly focused on the screen in front of me. Tasha and Ian's impending departures, Josh leaving YOU, and Daniel urging me to pitch agents lead to the thought: do I really like what I do? Or maybe with everything in store, it's time to consider other possibilities.

Chapter 22: My Eyes Are up Here

I stare out the patio French doors at brown leaves gliding over an autumn breeze. I used to associate autumn with last, wild surfing escapades, pumpkin spiced . . . every-goddamn-thing, and long, dusky evenings of multiple steaming coffee mugs and sketching. To me, this autumn seems to be about changes and good-byes. I can hardly believe that three whole weeks have swept by with me barely noticing, leaving me with less than a week to say a temporary yet still difficult good-bye to my Ian and Tash. In a way, it feels like every constant in my life is about to change, besides the most important one that is.

I turn to look at my constant sitting next to me, having a pleasantly silent dinner. I bring another forkful of salmon into my mouth, literally feeling Daniel's gaze on me. With my lips still closed around the fork, I trail my eyes up to his. He doesn't return my stare, given his eyes are practically burning a hole in my chest. I dip my chin, squinting to see if there's any couscous or sauce on my shirt. Nothing. I chance another glance his way. *Oh hi, the rest of me is also here.* The man seems to be in a boobies coma. Hypnotized by bosom.

I drop my fork to my plate, deliberately causing some clatter.

Nothing. I twist my mouth, staring at him. "D?"

"Hmm." His eyes not moving an inch.

"Daniel?"

"Yes, baby?" he tells my chest.

I lightly chuckle, my eyes narrowed at him. "Did I tell you, I had the Veyron newly painted in bright pink?"

"Mmmhmm . . ."

No? Really?

I fold my arms across the visually molested organs. Daniel, as though jerked out of a cozy dream, finally brings his eyes to mine.

I grin. "The salmon is delicious, ah?" He looks adorably flushed and muddled. I trap my smile with my teeth.

"Yeah, salmon." His eyes squint from my face to my chest. The creases between his brows deepen. "Hales?" He tips his chin my way. "Did you get a new bra or something?"

My brows turn to pucker. "No."

He nods. His eyes as though spellbound wind back in Boobyland. I leave my seat and head over to sit on him. "Hey, handsome, wanna cop a feel? You seem so fascinated, and anyhow, they are sort of yours."

The words are still fresh on my lips when Daniel's fingers come in contact with the skin under my shirt. "Damn right, they are." His fingers slowly graze up my ribcage, leaving raised skin in their wake.

"How would you feel if I didn't work for a while?" I ask, enjoying the feel of his fingers on me.

"Where's this coming from?" His attention shifts back to my face.

"I was thinking about starting to look for something else, explore other possibilities. Now that Josh is leaving and all. So it will probably take a while till I find something new."

His hands drop to hold either side of my waist. "Hales, you don't need to work at all. You know that." He squeezes my waist. "Just do whatever makes you happy."

"I never want to be that person. I don't ever want to rely on your money." I hold his stare.

"Our money." I can't help but notice the muscle above his jaw starting to tick.

"I'd feel more comfortable actually contributing to the "our" part." I air quote ours. An action that leads to an irritated headshake by my "placid and reasonable" husband-to-be. "Speaking of, I think we should sign a prenup before getting married."

"What are you trying to do?" His stare on me jumps from threat level low to severe in a blink of an eye. "The narrative this conversation is taking is starting to piss me off."

Looks like Dr. Jekyll will be joining us this fine evening.

"Can you listen for a sec?" The tone of my voice mirrors his brisk one.

He wipes his mouth with a napkin and tosses it onto his plate. "Not when you make no sense."

"Can you please explain to me how me looking out for your interests can be considered nonsense? Because I can't."

His features harden. "Because it implies a scenario in which we are not together, and that's something I'm not willing to discuss. Not even hypothetically."

I inwardly shake my head. "Believe me, it's the last thing I want, but what happens if for whatever reason we break up? What I bring to the table is a joke compared to . . ."

"Hayley, how can you say that?"

Uh oh, I'm Hayley now.

"How can you so easily dismiss everything you contribute?

How can money even be compared to a future together, affection, and children?" His lips purse. "And believe me, I don't see any situation in which I won't want you anymore. You're my future."

It's amazing how relentless and illogical he can sometimes be. *Always.* "What if . . . I don't know, something happens?"

"Hayley." It's a low warning.

"What if I were unfaithful?" *And how dumb I could sometimes be.*

I flinch at the wrath darkening his stare. "*Enough.*" He lifts me off him, rising to stand.

"Daniel?" I take a step back, watching him as he closes his eyes and takes a deep breath.

"Hayley, *drop it.* I'm done. I'm not taking part in this conversation anymore." He gives me a piqued glance and walks out of the room.

· · ·

"Idiot," I tell my reflection in the mirror. I grab my toothbrush and assault my teeth with vigorous brushing. Why couldn't I have handled it differently? Maybe avoid pressing the red button marked *Danger.* It's a poor excuse, but his stubbornness makes my logical wires short out.

Knowing him as well as I do, I decide to let him cool down a little. It's the best approach before resuming talks with any extremist party. I can't help but smile a little at the thought of how confident he is in me, in us. *He might love you as much, but you're still a complete idiot.*

I pull my shirt up over my head and toss it in the hamper. Cocking my head, I give my bra a curious examination. Daniel's mini obsession with my boobs earlier resurfaces as I frown at the way the hills of my breasts spill out of the cups. I send my hands to the clasp and take the bra off. Shrugging the straps down my arms, my frown deepens. My jiggling breasts are indeed fuller, and my nipples darker. I bring both hands to hesitantly feel them and am startled by the gasp leaving my lips. Boy, do I ignite. *The hell?* Tentatively, I bring my fingers to the pointed peaks. My eyes grow bigger at the sensation. My breasts are sensitive. As in *sensitive.* I touch them once more, and the first thing that jumps to my mind is how I wish it were Daniel's hands, mouth, skin, or Daniel's whatever, on me *right now*.

I push out a testy exhale, thinking about how we left things less than half an hour ago. Clearly, the current status-quo doesn't entitle jumping one another on a whim. This is not how you iron out disputes. Sensible people talk not grope. Disregarding the sensual buzz my body is transmitting, I head to bed.

I keep reading the same page over and over, but the content doesn't register. The author flawlessly portrays the story of a young girl's path from starvation to the Dutch parliament, but it's wasted on me. All I can think about is licking a path down Daniel's abs. Rereading how the brave girl pumps water from a well, the only thing I'm left with is the pumping. Which immediately nourishes the restless buzzing inside me. I close my eyes in frustration and all I see is Daniel. Naked. Sweaty. *Screw talking and settling our differences*. I reach for my phone and shoot out a message to the object of my desire.

When are you coming to bed?

Daniel: Later.

I roll my eyes. Time to be less testy and much more tasty, D.

How about now?

Daniel: I'm working.

Please come to bed?

Daniel: Are you done trying to pick a fight?

Oh, for goodness' sake.

Sorry for that.

Immediately, I send him the next message.

I'm sort of horny . . .

A grin spreads across my lips to the tramping of steps coming from the hall. The grin stretches into a radiant smile when Daniel appears in the doorframe. He slows down, looking at me, scratching his lips with his thumb.

"You were saying . . ."

In lieu of an answer, I push the covers aside. Looking at him from under my lashes, I send my hands to the hem of my shirt and pull it up. I don't wait for him to reach the bed to shimmy out of my panties. A lingered sigh of release leaves my mouth to the touch of his lips on my skin. There's a tough flair to the way he takes me next. Some sort of pleasure mixed with punishment, he is fierce and demanding, almost dominating. It's sensual and sinister and leaves me breathless, yet with a craving for more.

. . .

"You killed me, woman," Daniel says more than an hour later, making a whole production of crawling up the bed like some wounded soldier climbing out of a ditch. He drops onto his back next to me, catching his breath.

"Bless your philanthropic soul." I pat his bare chest, catching my own breath.

Daniel chuckles; damp clusters of hair cling to his forehead, his cheeks flushed with exertion. Still slumped on the bed, he cranes his neck to look at me, his cheek pressed into the mattress.

"Not that you'll ever, ever hear me complaining, but you were quite . . . demanding."

He grins at me.

"Can you really blame me?" I echo his smile and add, "Have you seen *you*?"

He sends his eyes to the ceiling. Sliding his hand under my lower back, he rolls me to lie on him. I kiss his lips through a smile. He chuckles into my kiss to the very blatant grumble coming from my stomach.

"Worked up an appetite projecting?" Daniel says to the room as I bury my smile in his chest.

"I could definitely eat." I tip up my head to look at him.

Not bothering with clothes, we make our way to the kitchen. I twist my lips from side to side, taking inventory of the profusion our fridge has to offer.

"How about all the food Nadine made?" Daniel asks from behind, leaning on the island, biting on an apple.

I shake my head, turning to face him. I don't think I'll ever get enough of his post-projecting looks. Bare, tanned chest, hair sticking in every possible direction, and a satiated glow. Inwardly patting myself on the back, I ask, "Do we have any beef jerky?"

Biting into the apple, Daniel shrugs in a how-the-hell-should-I-know manner. His eyes follow me as I turn to accost the pantry. "No beef jerky." I heave a peeved sigh.

Daniel cocks his head. "What's up with the face? It's only dried meat."

I frown at the odd craving I'm having trouble explaining. I'm not even that big on beef jerky in general. My mouth waters and I can almost taste the savory tang on my tongue. The look I give Daniel next must be of the desperate kind. Otherwise, I couldn't explain him grabbing his car keys and saying, "I'll go get you some."

"It's after midnight," I say, glancing at the oven's clock.

"Let me just get dressed," he says over his shoulder, halfway through the hall.

More than enjoying the sight of his muscled butt parading before me, I follow him into the bedroom. Shrugging on panties and a hoodie, I say, "I'll come with you."

Daniel buttons the last button of his jeans, pocketing his car keys. "That's what you're wearing?" He gestures at my bare legs with his hand.

"I'll stay in the car." I smile, stepping out of the room. "Let's take my car, though. It has butt warming."

"The owner's manual would probably disagree on the term." Daniel opens the passenger door for me. "It's a seat heater."

I smile to the window, enjoying the music as we pass by quiet streets. Daniel squeezes my hand. I turn to him, studying his concentrated profile. He sends me a sidelong glance and returns to look ahead at the dark road.

"I love you," I whisper, choked up with emotions.

He brings our joined hands to his lips, brushing mine gently with a kiss. "Love you," he says to my skin.

Less than ten minutes later, he rolls the car to a stop at an all-night gas station.

"Just beef jerky?" Daniel asks, holding the car door.

"Yes, please." I grin at him. I watch him as he steps out of the car. "Oh, and those . . ." One hand on the roof, he bends to look at me with a raised eyebrow, waiting. "What are they called? Those marshmallowy peanuts. Oh, circus peanuts."

Daniel gives me one, long assessing stare and nods. "Beef jerky and circus peanuts." Both a thin smile and a crease above the nose appear on his face.

"Here you go . . ." Daniel hands me the goods and opens a bottle of water for himself.

"God, they are so good." I relish the saltiness in my mouth.

Feeling Daniel's stare on me, I turn to face him. Utterly focused on my little midnight feast, I haven't noticed that he hasn't started driving. With the engine on, one hand on the wheel, he is turned my way, watching me enthralled.

I swallow the contents in my mouth. "What?" I beam at him.

His stare moves from my eyes to the open package of dried meat on one of my thighs to the ripped open bag of candy on my other. His eyes follow my hand as I bring a gummy peanut to my lips. "Hales?" he says somewhat contemplative. His eyes trade glances between the food on my thighs to my face before he asks, "Are you sure you're not pregnant?"

"You think I'm fat?" I swallow the candy; my voice wavers as my face falls. His expression turns from soft to somewhere along the lines of oh-no-I'm-engaged-to-a-nutjob. I drop my eyes to the strange food duet on my legs and take a deep breath. Everything about tonight runs through my head as I realize just how unbalanced I've been acting. It's as if I'm on auto-psycho this evening. I raise my eyes to Daniel, who's watching me attentively with a side smile. "I've been totally nuts tonight, uh?"

He nods. His smile broadening.

"Thanks for supporting all the crazy." I send him a timid smile.

"Always." He takes my hand in his. "Are you, though?"

"I don't think so. And I think it's too early to check this month."

He nods, giving me another weighing gaze before driving off.

Chapter 23: Last Meal Soirée

I smile to myself, enjoying Tash and Ian's animated gibe ping-pong. A trickle of sadness infiltrates my happy, turning my smile sentimental. This farewell dinner for my eternal soulmates has taken its toll on my emotions, to say the least. I'm a basket case, complete with my mood switching like an alternating current. I couldn't be happier for them both, and proud. Ian on the very promising path of living his dream, and Tash about to fast track up the corporate ladder while exploring new, exotic places. However, in the most selfish sense, I could not be more bummed.

"Told you, there are planes." My happy smile returns to Daniel's whisper in my ear. I tilt my head back to look up at him. Standing behind me, gazing down at me, he sends his hands to my shoulders. Squeezing gently, he rewards me with the softest of smiles. He bows down to leave a kiss on my lips. Still bent over me, he says, "For what it's worth, I'm not going anywhere."

"Promise?"

His answer is another kiss. A longer one.

"I think we're out of beer," Rafael says, drawing our attention.

"I'll get some more," Daniel says.

"I'll come with you." Rafael takes a step closer.

Hearing my name, I turn to Josh and Ian, catching up on their conversation. In my periphery, I notice Daniel replacing my sparkling wine with a glass of sparkling water. I turn to look at him in question. Holding the glass of wine in his hand, he subtly shakes his head. I roll my eyes only to be gifted with a beautiful smile and a wink.

"So many changes, uh?" Ian declares with enough drama that wouldn't fail a Hallmark movie. His eyes slowly move from me to Tasha, ending with Josh. After replenishing the booze supply, Daniel and Rafael left us to munch and talk while taking control of the grill. It's an impromptu dinner Tasha and I decided upon less than an hour ago while packing the last of Tasha's suitcases she'll be taking with her to Bangkok. Recalling Ian's response to the last-minute invite brings a smile to my face.

Ian: Mr. Josh Wild and Mr. Ian Tamura accept with great pleasure the kind invitation of Mrs. Idiot get hitched already, why don't you? and Mr. Hot-Stuff-Stark for the Last Meal Soirée, tonight at eight pm.

"The era of change." Tasha's voice matches Ian's melodramatic tone. I let out a light chuckle, causing Tasha to join me. "I don't think that we've been apart for this long since our undergrad days."

I sigh. "True."

"Weird." Tasha's turn to sigh.

"I have faith in you all. You'll manage." Josh smirks. Concurrently, three fries fly his way. Noticing our similar reaction, Ian, Tasha, and I beam at each other.

"Steaks, anyone?" Rafael places a plate of juicy steaks in the center of the table.

I'm not sure if it's the impending good-bye or my unstable mood, but the smell of grilled meat, which usually would have my mouth watering, has the very opposite effect. I snatch a bread roll from Ian's plate and tear a piece. I feel queasy and the bland taste of bread is the only thing remotely palatable. The elated conversation around me tunes down to the background as I space out, gazing at Daniel. He pushes up the sleeves of his black Henley, revealing his veiny forearms, ready to flip the burgers. He must sense my eyes on him as, tong in hand, he turns to look my way. Our eye lock feels more like an emotion because one can't feel as warm and loved by a stare alone. It's moments like this, the way we connect, that have me wishing I could be in his arms and never let go. Breaking our stare, he fetches his phone out of his pocket. A short glance at the screen and his placid air edges. *Must be work.*

"So Hales, how about you join us then?" Tasha's voice penetrates my Daniel gazing state.

"Ah?" I say, my mind still in Daniel land.

"Where are your etiquettes, gorgeous?" Ian quirks a brow, utterly amused. "Maybe wait with the eyeboning till your guests are gone."

Disregarding Ian, Tasha repeats her question. "Why don't you join Josh and Ian when they come to visits us?"

"Yeah, explore the Asian City of Sin with us, gorgeous mine." Ian grins.

"The only sin you'd be exploring is carby food," Josh says flatly.

"When is it happening?" I ask.

"We thought about letting them settle in first," Josh says.

"Sometime after the filming is done," Ian completes Josh's words. "In a few months, maybe."

Tasha's coaxing expression encourages me to say, "Sounds good. We could use a little vacation. I'll talk to Daniel." To my answer, the discussion turns into plans and excitement. I crane my neck, checking in on Daniel, only to find him still on the phone. Seeming troubled, he turns toward one of the guesthouses.

Chapter 24: Somewhere a Clock Is Ticking

Daniel

Taking a deep breath that does nothing to appease the increasing mayhem in me, I turn toward the guesthouses. Making sure I'm not in anyone's line of vision, I ask, "When?"

I shut my eyes, pinching my nose bridge. "Tomorrow? Why are you just now telling me about this?" I listen, my temper getting the better of me with each ticking moment. "I don't care what *you* think is best." Immediately regretting my lash out, I take a deep breath. "I'm sorry. When tomorrow?"

"It's okay," she says in a gentle voice. "At four."

"I'll be there."

She immediately objects.

"You don't get to decide that for me. I. Will. Be. There." I shake my head at her insistent attempt to convince me not to. "Please, don't argue with me."

She sighs heavily. "I love you."

I swallow hard over the pain in my chest. "Me too."

I take a step back to lean on the wall. Tipping my head back, I squeeze my eyes tight. The pounding in my head gains momentum. I try to compose myself with the rationale that at this point, I know nothing. We know nothing. I'm never one to speculate or jump to conclusions. I don't operate this way. I make a decision based on facts and logic, not assumptions. But somehow, this time, my gut feeling tells me I should worry. I'm well aware that any attempt to shake this off would be futile. *You've got to pull yourself together, Daniel, for Hayley's sake.* I can't have her go through anything that will break her heart. At least not for the time being.

I pocket my phone and take another deep inhale.

Glad to notice Rafael took over the grill in my short absence, I make my way back to Hales and her friends. Taking a seat next to Hayley, I notice her worrisome stare. I send her a side smile. She smiles back, but her eyes still assess me. I put my arm around her and pretend to take an interest in the conversation around me.

Throughout the evening, I do my very best to not appear as detached as I feel. Threading a sentence here or an expression there, I participate just enough not to raise concerns. Though the only thing I want is to lose myself in Hayley and drown everything else away.

More than an hour after everyone leaves, I'm still awake with Hayley sound asleep on my chest. I softly stroke her hair, breathing in her sweet cinnamon scent. I'm well aware of the sleepless night ahead, but at least, I have her in my arms. The only thing that has the power to, in a way, settle me and ease my mind.

Chapter 25: Every High Has a Come Down

I groan as the escalating sound of the alarm penetrates my deep sleep. Rubbing my eyes, I turn to search for Daniel. Hoping he's still around, I quickly put on a sweatshirt and make my way to the kitchen. A lukewarm, half-drunk coffee and the Veyron's keys missing from the bowl slightly bring me down. I was hoping to talk to him before he left for work this morning. Though he was as doting as ever, there was something about him last night I can't shake off. He seemed like something was weighing on him.

Trying to call him, I frown, realizing Daniel's phone is switched off. I toss my phone on the table and head back to the bedroom to get ready for work.

. . .

"I think it does a great job delivering the message," says our new intern.

Josh pushes his glasses up his nose and twists his mouth. "What do you think, Hayley?" Wheeling his chair back, Josh allows me a better view of the screen. We both examine the content for a stretch.

"I agree. The message is clearly transpired, but," I turn to Josh, "something about the background. To me, it's a bit too detailed. It takes too much of the attention."

Josh nods. "Maybe the text is enough. Leave the greyscale scheme." He points at the center of the monitor. "Hayley, let's have two drafts. One with the images faded out and one without the images completely. Skip the next meetings; I'd like to have it ready this afternoon."

I nod, more than thankful to be spending the next few hours buried in work.

With a fresh cup of coffee by my side, I dive right into the InDesign program, blocking out the busy office buzz around me.

By the time the big green clock on the wall turns four, I'm finally able to leave my desk. Feels like the day has flown by. Only now, stretching, waiting for Josh's feedback on the final drafts I've sent him, I realize I haven't eaten anything today.

I grab my purse and drop by Josh's office. I pop my head in his room. "I'm going to grab something to eat. Do you want me to get you anything?"

He lifts his head above his screen. "No thanks, I'm good. Great job on the Road Trip drafts, I think we'll go with the clean-cut one."

I nod. "It's classier. So I'll be back in thirty. I'll be on my phone if you need me."

My mouth literally waters as I unwrap my roasted beetroot and goat cheese sandwich. Looking out the window of the cozy sandwich shop, I enjoy every bite of my late lunch. I take a generous sip of the sweet tea, trying to call Daniel again. I frown when I discover he still has his phone switched off. Searching for his PA's number, I notice two new email notification in my private inbox. The first one is yet another formal representation rejection, and the other makes me swallow hard on my next sip. I set the beverage aside and reread the email.

Hello Hayley,

I've reviewed your illustrations sample and I'm very intrigued. I'd like to discuss representation. When would be a good time to call?

Thanks very much. I look forward to hearing from you.

All the best,

Terry Henson

Orange Illustration Agency

Holy shiz! Filled with excitement, I reply to the email. Beaming, I reach for my sandwich. Halfway through my next bite, my phone hollers. My forehead wrinkles at the unfamiliar number on my screen. My tentative, "Hello," soon dissolves into a stream of introductions and compliments coming from the other end of the line.

"Nice to meet you too, Terry. And wow, thank you. I'm humbled."

The agent hardly lets me string a syllable, telling me how much she liked my work. When she says she thinks it will be a perfect fit to an upcoming children book, I drop the sandwich in my hand. I swallow hard, stunned. Here I was excited about someone interested in representing me and connecting to my work, but an actual job?

"Hayley, are you there?" Terry says to my silent pause.

"Yeah. I'm just. Yes, sure, Thursday sounds perfect."

I stare at the phone in my hand, trying to grasp the last five minutes. A smile spreads across my face as the realization sinks in. I ask for the bill and leave a generous tip, beaming at the waiter. High on excitement, I make my way back to the office. My fingers prickle at the thought of trying Daniel's number again. I can't wait to share the news with him and on a whim decide to go visit him at the office right after work.

Chapter 26: Wherefore Art Thou, D?

I pass by the coffee shop below the Stark Software offices to get Daniel his favorite before climbing up to his office. I frown back at Anne's frown when she sees me. Acentric and uptight as she usually is, she'd always been nice to me. Even a bit too trying, but she always means well, bless her neurotic soul. "Is he with someone?" I ask tipping my chin at Daniel's closed door. Her frown deepens and she jumps out of her chair. "I brought him coffee." I gesture with the cup in my hand.

"Miss Grace, um."

"It's Hayley," I murmur. Not sure why I even bother anymore. It's a lost cause.

Her brows almost meet when she says, "Mr. Stark didn't come in today." She looks at me. "I thought he was at home actually. His phone has been switched off since early morning."

I try to search my mind to remember if Daniel mentioned anything about being away.

"He had a full day. He didn't even let me know he was going to be absent or ask me to cancel his meetings."

What's going on, D?

"I see," I say, not sure what to think. Trying hard not to let the worry seeping into me grow, I say, "I'm heading home, so I'll ask him to call you when I see him."

On my way to the car, I go through my emails again. With Daniel's constant traveling, we got to the point where he just forwards me his itineraries, instead of telling me about them. There's nothing planned for today.

With my handbag still on my shoulder, I pass by each room, including the guesthouses, finding them all empty. I plunge onto one of the kitchen's highchairs, my mind working overtime. I drop my bag on the counter, my shoulders slumping with the weight of my worry. The more I think about it, the less sense it makes. Erratic as he may be at times, he'd never just up and disappear without letting me know he'd be gone for a while. Or let Anne know, for that matter. She practically runs his life. I try not to wander into worrisome territory. Pushing out of the chair, I make my way to change into something warmer.

It's not okay to sit in one place and delve for hours on end. It's not okay to sulk for the equivalent amount of time. It's not okay to feel such healthy belligerence toward your significant other without a sound reason. And it's definitely not okay to screen your best friends' calls. But that's exactly what I've been doing since I got home. I chance a glance at my phone's clock. *Nine thirty. D, where are you?* As much as I try, I can't tune out the whispers of our recent "hiccups," and the very vivid dream I had hums in the recesses of my mind. My stomach is so strung, I feel nauseated. I curl on the living room sofa, wrapping a throw around me, waiting. Somehow, our home in a way still feels warm by his presence, yet painfully cold by his absence. Fatigue laced dread sneaks in, slowly and heavily pressing on my eyelids.

Shaken, my eyes rip open at the chime of my phone. For short, hazy moments, I'm disoriented, surfacing from a brief, tense doze. Relief washes over me to Daniel's name on the screen.

"Daniel," his name is an urgent breath.

"Hales . . ."

I used to think love was an urban legend and that you could never be that connected to another person. But now I know it couldn't be truer and that that person lives in your bloodstream and you come to know them so deeply that simply the cadence of their voice can shake your entire world with dread.

"Are you okay?" is blurted out of my mouth.

"Yes. Can you come down to Baja?"

Baja? "What? Baja? When? What are you doing in Baja?"

"You're booked on the next flight going out at half past ten. Hales, I can't talk right now. Just come."

And he is gone.

Jarred to my core, I stare ahead, holding the phone in a tight grip. I blink twice and drop my eyes to the device. It's hard to comprehend the nature of my emotions, I'm burning from the inside—part anxious, part mad. Not sure which part is greater.

Chapter 27: Come Pick Me Up

The moment the plane's wheels come in contact with the ground, I try Daniel's number once more. Nothing. Mixed emotions swim in my head, weighing on my stomach. *Don't go there, Hales.* The fear and anxiety throw me back to when he was held hostage in Thailand. At least, this time, I know for sure where he is, and most importantly, that he's alive. This time, besides harboring tension that makes it hard to properly breathe, I'm also mad. Because whatever it is that he needs to tell me, he could have done it in so many different and better ways. Talk to me, confront me, instead of letting me jump into the rabbit hole that is my imagination. Feels like in a way, we're back to when we started seeing each other when he kept everything to himself. This is something I'm not willing to endure again. Not anymore, especially at this point in our relationship when we're planning a future together, a family.

Sitting in the cab, I stare at the scenery passing before me, not really seeing it. My mind, fueled by worry and irritation, doesn't take anything in besides the thoughts twirling in my head. I heave loudly, shaking my head. I'm upset. Majorly upset. Because whatever he needs to tell me, he shouldn't have made me come all the way to Baja to do it. With only moments left of the drive, I start composing the mother of all lectures in my head. But no matter how mad I am, I'll be there for him, whatever it is. I just hope he still wants me to be there for him . . .

I believe that we all possess an innate intuition of what's right and what's wrong for us. How we choose to utilize that intuition is a different story. For me, I've disregarded it many times, or occasionally even defied it. Alas, very seldom, I have embraced it. However, when it comes to Daniel and our relationship, the moment I chose to put that ring on my finger, I took an internal oath to trust my feelings for him, my intuitions, our bond, and mostly, his love for me. In the same breath, I also pledged to toss my insecurities into the garbage and pay less attention to the pinch of maddening traits my beloved psycho has been blessed with. Because, boy, since the tsunami that is my Daniel has barged into my life, I've been both Danielized, and to a degree, let's call a spade a spade, stupefied. Vowing to first listen and then lash out, I pay the driver and search for my key.

The key isn't necessary, though, for the front door is unlocked. I feel my way through the dark till my hand reaches the light switch. I give the living room a peep and cringe at the half bottle of scotch standing solo on the table. I pick up Daniel's shirt that's lying on the floor next to his deserted shoes. I drop the shirt on the armrest, and head toward where blurry music is playing.

"Daniel," I call out, still nursing confusion, and to a greater degree, anger. I'm more than ready to confront him with everything that has been boiling inside me for the past twenty-four hours. A quick glance at the panoramic windows reveals his whereabouts. My heart lodges up in my throat as I make my way to the deck. The only light illuminating the space is the full moon's soft gleam. The background music is loud and angry, pounding in perfect harmony to my heart. I take a couple of steps toward the outdoor surround system and turn the volume down. That's when Daniel finally realizes I'm there.

The look in his eyes as they shine from under the cowl of a hoodie makes my next breath trap inside. I study him for a stilled moment, slouched on a recliner, clad in a dark hoodie and board shorts. He opens his mouth to speak and shuts it right back, a frown, painful frown, veiling his face. I take another step, eyes steady on his, fearing to hear what was about to leave his mouth. The air he is radiating makes me want to both hug him tight and run the other way, as fast as I can. The look on his face tells me that whatever he is about to say will break my heart because that's exactly how *he* looks. Wrecked. I take another hesitant step to reach him. He tips his head to look up at me, and I physically feel his pain filtering into me.

I part my lips to speak but no words come out. Instead, I'm being pulled forward by his arm that's encircling my waist. "Hales," leaves his mouth as he buries his face in my stomach. Instinctively, my fingers thread in his hair, holding him to me in compassion. I bend down to kiss his hair, my eyes closed, my heart pelting at the walls of my chest. I let him take comfort in me for a silent beat.

"Daniel," I say in a dainty voice. "What is it? You're scaring me." It feels like a small ice cube is making its way slowly down my neck as I wait for him to speak.

He looks up, his features hard, the creases between his brows dense. "Iris's cancer is back."

"No," is ripped out of my throat. A watery screen blurs my vision as I stare back at Daniel.

"The results came in today," he says, overwhelming sadness sitting in his eyes.

"I-I'm so sorry," I stutter, gazing back at him through unshed tears.

Daniel pulls me onto his lap, embracing me tightly, burying his face in my hair.

We hold one another closely in this darkness, between periods of brief conversations and stretched silence. Daniel answers the questions I have after he explains Iris's disease and the series of treatments she has ahead of her.

He also told me about a long and exhausting argument they had, where he'd implored she move to San Francisco, at least for the treatments. In utter frustration, he tells me how she wouldn't cave in.

"Hey." I send my hand to his bristled cheek. "You should have told me about it from day one."

He shakes his head, jaw clutched. "You had enough weighing on you. I didn't want to add any additional tension."

It's my turn to shake my head. "It doesn't work like this. There I was prioritizing me before you and I didn't even notice you were going through something so grave. I mean, I didn't think that there was something in addition to the regular daily stress." I let out a bitter chuckle. "Daniel, I came here tonight ready to give you a piece of my mind, not even knowing you were . . ."

"You came here for me, Hales. That's all that matters." His fingers trace over my freckles, over the bridge of my nose. He leans in to lightly kiss the trail.

I look at him, holding his stare with mine. "Because you always take precedence, no matter what." His eyes soften. "I love my family and friends, but nothing comes close to what you mean to me. I'll always be there for you. I can't do that if I don't know what you're going through, though. You need to let me in."

"I needed to process it by myself. Hales, I can't even measure how important you are to me, but this is something that . . ." He heaves loudly. "Fuck. I didn't . . . Hales, I don't know how to deal with it. I can't lose her." He closes his eyes. "It's so hard going through this again." He shakes his head. "It's amazing how helpless I feel. Everything I own, all the money in the world, is worth nothing when you can't use it to help the people important to you."

"You are not helpless. You're there for her and that is all that matters. And, this time, I'm here for you," I say in a soft voice. I hold him tight, the lump in my throat expanding. *There's only you for me. You and so many feelings.*

Chapter 28: Keep Your Chakras Lit

My breath becomes shaky as soon as the door opens. Noticing my quivering lips, Iris takes me into her arms. "Hayley, honey." She leans her chin on my shoulder, hugging me with candid warmness.

Releasing me, she gives Daniel a long scan. "You haven't slept." She slowly slides the palm of her hand over his unshaven cheek, looking at him with loving eyes.

"I'm okay," he says curtly. "How do you feel?"

Her stare lingers on him, assessing. "I'm fine. It's you I worry about. Come on in. I'll start the kettle."

I lace my fingers with Daniel's, bringing our joined hands to my lips. His lip tips up in a weary smile as he returns my stare, sitting next to me on the low sofa.

A jingling sound of a few bell anklets approaches. "I missed you greatly, Hayley," Iris says, setting a round tray with an intricately textured teapot and small plates of dried fruits and oatmeal cookies on the table. She settles herself cross-legged on a patchwork bean bag, facing us.

"Same here." I smile at her, working hard not to show the sadness inside me.

"So tell me, what's new?" Her perpetual thin smile on as she pours us tea. Her hands hug the mug, her eyes caressing me.

"Oh, nothing much. How are you?" I say, too devastated to be acting business as usual.

I turn to look at Daniel, who's drinking from his steaming mug. My brows crinkle. Daniel doesn't drink tea, ever. But clearly he's not himself. He appears to be . . . lost.

"Well, I'm going to have my first exhibition in three months," she beams, her eyes weak yet joyful.

"That's wonderful," I say. I'm genuinely thrilled for her but still can't refrain from thinking how she'll incorporate it with her forthcoming chemo and the side effects.

Her stare becomes dreamy as she says, "Having your art up there in person for people to see . . ."

"Maybe you should wait with that," Daniel's grave voice stops her. "Wait till the first round of chemo is over. You'll need all your strength to heal. I'm not sure if now is the best time to put yourself under additional pressure."

She shakes her head, her soft smile intact. "I'm not going to stop everything I believe in and love, not even for a while. To win a fight, you should take the bad with the good. Balance, love. It's all about balance. This couldn't have come at a better time, as I see it. I have something to look forward to. Something to take my mind off things I don't want to give too much weight to."

"Iris." Her name on Daniel's lips is a concern, a struggle.

"I've been there before," she says, and the effect of her words bluntly shows on Daniel's face. He looks in pain. "I got through it once, and I'll do that again." She inches to touch his hand. "You shouldn't worry so much."

It appears as if he is doing everything in his power not to explode. "Someone needs to take this seriously." He sighs. "At least, move in with us till you're better."

"Let us take care of you," I add.

She shakes her head again. "I appreciate your offer and love, but my life is here. I'm happy here, and I have so many things going on. I'm not going to drop everything and focus on my illness. You should never give up and stop believing because that's when you can taste the end."

"Iris," I try.

"Honey ..." She shakes her head, her lips in an easy smile. "I need to be somewhere where I feel spiritually fitted. Spiritually balanced."

From the corner of my eye, I notice Daniel's fuse slowly burning. He's one chakra talk away from detonating. I lean into him, take his hand in mine, and hold it between my hands. He sends his other hand to fiddle with a pale green sticky note stuck to the low table. He tilts his head reading it. He frowns, turning his stare to his mother. "All things are the truth in themselves?"

"Just a reminder of the Buddhist Lotus Sutra." Iris says. The frown in Daniel's expression deepens, that burning fuse shifting gears. "It's so magnificent, how the universe sends us exactly what we need when we need it the most, don't you think?" She adds next.

We both give her a "are you high, woman?" look.

Her smile expands. "Remember Dr. Owen, honey?" she asks Daniel.

"Of course." He turns to me. "That's the doctor I had her see. He's supposed to be the best."

"We started seeing each other," Iris says in her calm, singsong voice. I let out a small chuckle. Loving her a little more than I already do. Only Iris can find the good in a fatal disease and applause the forces to be for it.

"Oh, for fuck's sake. You've got to be kidding me." Yep, that's Daniel's patience finally wearing thinner than thin. "I'm going to . . ." He gestures with his phone to nowhere in particular, standing up.

Oh, D, aren't you going to hold hands with us and praise the universe?

I bite on my lip, watching Daniel make himself scarce. Iris turns to me, shaking her head, amusement donning her hazel eyes.

"So tell me all about this doctor."

Her eyes spark up. She takes a throw pillow and places it on her thighs. Fiddling with the ruffled hem, she says, "He has such a kind spirit." Sass climbs up onto her lips. "And he's all kinds of handsome."

"I'm intrigued." I perk up, not able to subdue my smile.

"Well, after my biopsy, he asked me for coffee. The same evening we went out for dinner. That evening lasted till the next day." My grin widens to her wink. "We've been seeing each other since."

"That's wonderful. I'm so happy for you." It amazes me how her dreadful disease doesn't even factor into her overall state. She looks genuinely content. Taking a sip of my drink, I wait for her to carry on.

"Hayley darling, you can't believe how a good orgasm frees your mind of everything pressing."

Spraying out the tea, I look at her horrified. In the same breath, I thank all possible spiritual beings that Daniel wasn't present for his mother's unabashed declaration.

"It works miracles," she adds.

How does one answer such a declaration from one's future mother-in-law? "Oh, I couldn't agree more, and thank you *for spawning such an orgasm-giving extraordinaire yourself. Great job! Here's to freeing orgasms!"*

My cheeks cool down a little when I finally say, "Um, I'm glad you've found ways to ease your mind of things. Good for you."

Chapter 29: I Kissed a Girl

Saying that the past few weeks have been easy would be a complete falsehood. They've been eventful and stressful and tense. Albeit, if I'm being completely honest, there have also been little comforting sparks of joy that have helped in keeping my mental balance to a certain degree.

Sitting at my desk, wrapping up a presentation Josh asked me to put together, I smile at the thought of the last time Ian and I had joined Iris for her chemo. It was a day before Ian was supposed to leave again after a short visit. Given his great fondness for Iris, he insisted on tagging along. Sucking on popsicles, taking *Cosmo* love and relationship quizzes together, we could hardly contain our spurts of laughter. By the fourth question, two more patients joined our little hoopla. When three more ladies showed interest in taking part, I had to run to the nearest convenience store to get some more popsicles. We took turns answering the questions, each one of us spicing up our answers for the sake of women comradery and amusement. There was a moment of collective feminine, and one Ian, swooning, when Owen, Iris's doctor boyfriend, came to say hi.

By the time the session was about to end, each and every one of the ladies was more than a little in love with Ian. *Who can really blame them?*

When Daniel dropped by to pick us up, Ian declared, gesturing at Daniel, "See what I mean?" Daniel's expression grew uncomfortable to Iris's wide, proud grin and the "mmmhmm," and "you go, girl!" announced my way from the rest of the gaggle. Noticing his jaw starting to work, I wrapped my hand around his waist. Leaning in, I whispered, "Take one for the team. Wow them with that smile of yours, pretty boy." Shaking his head, Daniel nodded, his side smile making an appearance.

When Daniel took Iris's stuff, helping her to the car, I had to literally pull Ian away from his insta-fans. "Can't wait for the movie to come out," followed us as we stepped out of the clinic.

I reread the notes I added to the email for Josh, making sure there are no glitches or forgotten items. I press send and rise to stand, walking to the office kitchen, deliberately putting off tackling my next task. I take extra time stirring sugar into my coffee and talking to my colleagues.

With a bittersweet sense of closure, I stroll back to my cubicle. The fact that soon enough Josh will be leaving too makes typing my resignation letter a bit less melancholic. Saying good-bye to something you are attached to and mostly enjoyed, no matter what's coming next, is always sad. And just like that, the notion of Tasha and Ian being away filters in, tears welling in my eyes. Again? *Really, Hayley?* Seems like my pastime of preference these days is weeping. *I* can't even stand the emotional mess I've become. As of late, I can't even fathom where and when it'll strike. Saying good-bye to my friends, being there for Iris in her hour of need, listening to a song, Daniel giving me his special smile, *watching a damn toilet paper commercial featuring little puppies*, and I turn into a pitiful bag of tears. I blame it on the volatility of the past months. So many changes in such a short time make it hard to come out unscathed.

I shake off the meditative state when a sound signals a message on my phone. An involuntary giggle flies out of my mouth as I read Ian's text.

Ian to Tasha and Hayley: I kissed a girl and I didn't like it. Blargh, the taste of cherry ChapStick. Being a movie star is not as simple as y'all commoners think it is.

I text back. **I'm truly sorry for your misfortune. Wishing you everything you need during this difficult time.**

Ian to Tasha and Hayley: Y'all women are so warm and soft and slimy.

Inwardly chuckling, I shoot out the next text. **Which one of her lips did you have to kiss exactly?**

Ian to Tasha and Hayley: I'm appalled, young gorgeous. I'm about to retch all over the set.

An answer from Tasha doesn't take long to arrive.

Natasha to Ian and Hayley: Taking offense on behalf of the female population, especially the cherry ChapStick users. Oh and for Katie Perry in particular for her beautiful song not just being plagiarized but tarnished.

Ian to Tasha and Hayley: Don't you type at me in that tone of voice, young lady!

Not a second passes and another text from Ian comes. This one is a selfie of his lips puckered into a kiss.

I'm still grinning widely when Josh pops his head in my cubicle. "What's so funny?"

"Ian," I say with a "who else?" expression.

He nods with a smile. "What has he done now?"

"Nothing that's outside the gray area of the law."

"Phew." Josh exhales with a melodramatic press of his hand to his chest.

I grin and show him the photo of Ian's kiss on my phone. He shakes his head with a smitten smile. *Oh, young love. Bound in thy rainbow flag. Apologize for this, Lord Byron, but it really fit the moment.*

"Saw your email. That's it, eh?" Josh says. I take a deep breath, bobbing my head. "Let's go for a celebratory something sweet."

"Sounds perfect." I stand, following him to reception.

Chapter 30: Perfect Sense

Daniel heaves loudly, righting his sitting position next to me, leaning on the headboard. He rubs his palm over his morning scruff. "Hales, let's just set a date already, for fuck's sake." I turn to him with a start. *Good morning to you too, psycho.* I'm afraid to ask what he dreamed about, waking up all tickled pink.

"I haven't had coffee yet," I murmur, my stomach contracting at the thought of coffee. *Blargh. Blargh, coffee? BLARGH, COFFEE?* What's happening to me? All the new, odd sensations that have been taking over my body lately parade into my mind, drums and all, enkindling an epiphany. The tiny nudging feeling in my lower belly, my tender breasts, the faint sense of nausea that never leaves. *Oh I know, I know perfectly well where this blargh coffee must be coming from.*

"I want you officially mine. It's been over almost a *goddamn* year." Daniel's eyes narrow at me.

"Oh, I am yours, believe me, now more than ever . . ." *God, it's so warm in here.* I rise to sit, maybe a bit too quickly. The room spins for an excruciating moment. Oh, crap, I'm going to hurl. I lift one finger and bolt to the bathroom, not even able to close the door behind me. I fall to my knees and before I'm able to open my mouth and let all things wreaking havoc in my stomach out, Daniel drops to the floor behind me. He holds my hair back as I dip down, and with immense cramps, let it all out. Light sweat covers my forehead by the third time my stomach constricts and fluids gush out of me. *So romantic, it's almost lyric.*

I wipe my mouth with toilet paper and move to lean on the cold tiled wall. Raising my head, I close my eyes and inhale, working to get back to normal.

"Hales, what's wrong?" I open one eye to his hazel concern. Daniel inches up toward the sink and comes right back with a damp rag. He runs the cooling fabric gently over my forehead, above my lips. His other hand stroking my hair. "If that's your reaction to getting married, it sort of bruises my ego," he teases, causing me to crack a pale smile. "Baby, you okay?"

I nod. "I just need a moment," I say in a weak voice. Daniel's features tighten with concern as he runs the cloth over my forehead once more.

Not exactly how I planned it. *Ready, D?* I inwardly shake my head at the moment. "I always imagined I'd tell you this in a more ceremonial-esque kind of way, candles, sea, music, doves, fireworks, you know, full-on schmaltz." He cocks his head, his eyes running over my, I can only assume, green around the gills, face. "God, I must look like a disaster, but well, here goes. . ." I sigh, feeling miserable. Feeling the same as I probably look right now. *Pregnancy glow, my bum.* "I-I'm pregnant . . . I think."

Daniel's lips part for a magical moment in which he couldn't appear more handsome, shocked, and confused. He blinks at me. "Hales, I always think you're the most beautiful woman I've ever seen, but you've never looked as beautiful as you are right now."

"*Really*? Now's the time to be making fun of me, when I'm miserable?" I shake my head. "Bad timing, dude."

His lips don't lift an inch, on the contrary, solemnity suffuses his features. "Hales." His voice is warm and rich. "You are so beautiful like that, with my child inside of you."

Me? Melting into a frothing puddle. My lately quick-on-the-trigger emotions brim, welling my eyes. "You can't say things like that." I wipe a tear. "I'm pregnant, I can't handle it." Daniel's lips arch; his eyes join the dancing. "Daniel Stark, father of my unborn baby, will you marry me . . . soon?" I look at him from under my damp lashes.

His grin turns radiant. "Get your ass up now and rinse your mouth so I can kiss you." He bends to kiss my forehead with a smile. Not waiting for me to follow orders, he lifts me up and settles me on the vanity. Our joyful eyes latch as Daniel hands me a small cup of mouthwash. Standing between my thighs, beaming, he watches me as I spit out the solution as gracefully as I can into the sink.

I wipe my mouth with a towel he hands me. "We're so romantic; someone should turn our story into a book." I toss the towel on the granite plank.

Daniel lightly chuckles, his hands cupping my cheeks. "Can you shut up for a second and let me kiss you?"

Humor dissolves into fragile tenderness when our lips connect. My heart aches so sweetly when he tilts his head, brushing his lips ever so caringly over mine. "I love you so much," he says. His warm breath carrying the words into me. His hands slide to my waist, hugging me closer to him, his mouth never leaving mine. I lean in, pressing against him, my hands caressing his warm skin. Melting into his embrace, into him.

A new wave of nausea prompts me to break the magic. "Sorry." I push him back, jumping off the vanity. I put the toilet lid down after vomiting whatever was left in me.

"Come here." Daniel helps me nestle between his legs, where he leans against the wall by my side. I rest my head back on his chest, letting him cover me with his warmth. "Better now?"

I nod, too weak to speak. Tightening his embrace around me, he rests his chin on my hair.

"What did you mean when you said you *think* you're pregnant? Haven't you taken a test?"

"Oh, I'm pretty sure I am. There are too many signs to indicate otherwise. But I will see my OB/GYN, just to make it official and make sure everything's okay. But you know what, why don't I take one right now? Do you mind getting me one from the upper drawer?"

Daniel eases to stand, helping me to my feet. He takes a couple of steps to reach the vanity. Opening the drawer, he pivots my way. Query covers his handsome face. "How many of these did you get?"

I wince. There must be about fifteen untouched home pregnancy test packets scattered around the small drawer. Originally, there were eighteen, back before Ian insisted we detect the presence of pregnancy hormones in our bodies. I bite my lip. "Hmm, a few?"

"And never used them?" Daniel adds, assessing me with a confused side smile.

"Didn't want to obsess about it."

"Oh, that makes perfect sense." He shakes his head, his lips set in a smirk.

Chapter 31: Roasted Bird and News

Three months later

"Can you stop inhaling the appetizers?" I swat Ian's hand away from the truffles pesto crostini dish.

"What? I'm just being sympathetic to you and your condition. I'm eating for two." He manages to snatch another crostini in a steal the ball stealth maneuver.

"Of course, you are," Tasha breathes, taking a sip of her champagne. "Doesn't look like you eat much." She gives my tight red woolen dress a scan.

"I don't. I practically have to force myself to eat." I set the rest of the food Nadine so artfully crafted onto serving platters.

"That rack, though." Tasha shakes her head with attitude. "Damn girl, you're sizzling."

A short giggle leaves my mouth. The smile stays on my lips with the memory of Ian noticing my figure earlier this evening, seeing me for the first time in three months when he and Josh arrived at our Kith and Kin Thanksgiving dinner.

Daniel opened the door to them, and I followed right after. Entering the foyer and noticing me, Ian did a double take. In a production that wouldn't fail Tarantino, he took a couple of steps back to examine the nonexistent door plaque. "Say, Josh, are you sure we're at the right address?" The three of us eyed him in unison. "I thought we were going to dinner at the Stark residence, and here we are at the Playboy mansion."

I was the first one to decode The Ian, given my seniority in dealing with his uniqueness and the fact that his eyes were practically burning holes in my bosom. Being the devout fan of the recent changes in my figure, Daniel was the next one to acknowledge Ian's words with a healthy chuckle. Daniel has been following the transformation of my body from skinny to Playboy bunny padded with utter fascination. Due to a combination of morning sickness and hormones, my waist has shrunken while the girls, on the other hand, broke all barriers and let loose.

Daniel shook Josh's hand while Ian wrapped his arms around me. "Gorgeous, you look all kinds of stunning and sexy. I missed your face."

"I missed you something fierce," I whispered into his ear, my eyes starting to water while I inwardly cussed. "Damn you, ruthless hormones, this is really getting old."

Ian eased out of our embrace, holding me by my shoulders and scanning me from up close. "They are like puffy clouds. I want to rest my head on them and take a nap. Can I touch them?" A mischievous smile adorned his lips.

A slap on his back, stronger than was called for, interrupted our moment. "Let's get drinks," Daniel said in a voice holding warning. Josh grinned and I rolled my eyes, following them into the living room.

"When are your parents and Steven getting in?" Tasha asks, bringing me back to the present.

"Soon. They were supposed to meet Iris at the airport and

commute together. Daniel arranged for a car to pick them all up."

"Ready to tell your dad the good news?" Ian says, trading stares with Tasha first, and then moving to me. I sigh and rest my hip on the kitchen island.

"Oh c'mon, he'll be thrilled. He'll get over all the rest. I bet he will." It's Tasha sprinkling some holiday spirit to the air.

"I know my dad. He'll be thrilled, that's for sure. But I can assure you he won't be that big on the whole baby before marriage concept, to say the least. Not to mention what he'll do to Daniel."

"You can send Daniel to me right after. I'll be more than glad to lick his wounds." Tasha and I push Ian's chest. Nearly losing his balance, he wobbles backward. "What? I'm just trying to be a Good Samaritan."

"Be a Good Samaritan by getting all of these to the table." I gesture with my chin at the profusion of delectable food on the island. Though we hired Nadine to take care of the menu for tonight, I've decided not to hire staff to help with serving. Everyone invited means so much to me, and I wanted to keep it intimate. Daniel raised his concern about me working too hard or stressing. When Tasha and Ian assured him they would help, he finally relented. I swear, if he could have his way, I'd be wrapped up in bubble wrap all day only for him to unwrap come bedtime.

"Hales?" Daniel's voice reaches us from the living room, followed by elated greetings. Tasha and Ian give me encouraging smiles.

Tasha squeezes my shoulder. "Oh, don't worry. Worst case, we'll celebrate Thanksgiving by either bailing Daniel or your dad out."

The three of us snort in stereo. "Nothing like creating fond memories," I say and start toward our guests.

One look at my mother and I know she knows. She watches us

with a sentimental smile and glossy eyes as Daniel and I stand before them. We asked them to join us on the patio, opting for some privacy in delivering the news, even though most of the guests present already know. It's not that I didn't want to tell my parents, I couldn't wait to do just that, but I preferred to do it face to face.

With his hand enlaced around my waist, Daniel starts. "Thank you for coming. We're glad to have you here with –"

Too excited and fidgety, I cut him off, exclaiming, "We're expecting a baby."

The watery screen in my mom's eyes turns into waterworks. "Oh, Lelly." I'm swallowed into her vanilla and home scented hug. She kisses my cheeks, holding me long. She turns to give Daniel the same emotion-saturated treatment. Daniel chuckles, somewhat discomforted by the teary kisses attack.

My dad takes a step toward me, edginess and excitement playing on his face. He takes me into his arms, resting his chin on the crown of my head. "Congratulations, Lelly." His hand moves to smooth my hair. "Are you feeling well? You should be taking prenatal vitamins. And FGF – your iron has always been low, and now, more than ever, you should take care of that."

"I got it covered, Dad. My doctor is pretty strict. And believe me, Daniel is very concerned about my diet. He has a chef to cook healthy food for me."

Overtly, my dad disregards my last comment. "If you suffer from morning sickness, you should get some ginger candy. They come highly praised."

"Dad." I ease back to meet his eyes. "It's Daniel's baby too," I whisper.

"Right. It is." He nods. Stone-faced, he turns to Daniel. Holding his hand out, he says, "Congratulations, Daniel."

Daniel shakes his hand, "Thank you, Dr. Grace."

My dad's eyes are hard on Daniel. "Work keeping you busy?" My brows furrow at the odd question. "You haven't found the time to marry my daughter. She not important enough to do it the right way or are you still keeping your options open?" I wince. Daniel throws me a look that feels more like a whip cracking.

"Dad, it was actually me. I'm the one who has been postponing the wedding. If Daniel could have it his way, we'd have been married a long ago."

"You always let Hayley take the heat for you?"

My mom and my words collide as we exclaim, "Derek Grace!" "Dad!"

"Hales." Daniel turns to me. "Why don't you help your mom get settled in. I'd like to talk with your dad." He caresses my cheek. "We'll join you soon." He leaves a kiss on my forehead. Reluctant, I give my dad a scolding look and walk my mom into the house.

. . .

Ian sighs dramatically. "Occupational hazard." Iris's smile brightens, waiting for him to go on about how during the filming of an intimate scene, his co-star sneezed and he had to jump back to not, as he puts it, get any of her germs into his system. By the jerk of his body, his arm flailed back, causing his pinky to brush against a lit candle. "A second-degree burn." His dour headshake backs the severity of his traumatic injury.

"We're glad you made it in one piece after all, soldier," Tasha says to her tall glass, eliciting fond laughter from Josh, Rafa, and me.

"Not all of us just sit on the beach all day long, sip Mai Tais, and call it work, Tash."

Tasha, unfazed by Ian's dig, says, "Oh, I wish it could only be that way." Her cheeks develop into a ruddy hue by Daniel's eyes on her. "I mean…" She straightens in her seat. "I'm not complaining. The work is great, it's just . . ."

Ian snorts, his face alight with mischief. "Stammer much, Barbie?"

I give both Ian and Tash a "behave, kids, or there's no dessert" look to which they both roll their eyes and right after trade an amused glance. *Kids, sometimes it's all about attention.*

Daniel chuckles and turns to resume his conversation with Steven. A warm fuzzy feeling powders my belly at how well my brother and Daniel get along. When Daniel offers for Steven to stay at the Baja house with his friends for their upcoming break, my smile grows at my father's failed attempt to hide his complacency.

"So, Natasha darling, how is Thailand? I've wanted to go there forever, but somehow, Derek and I always end up vacationing in Boca Raton." My mom shrugs; the apples of her cheeks rosy and her eyes shining.

"It's unlike any place I've been to before," Tasha says, smoothing her deep midnight mini velvet dress. "In the best of ways. At first, I was overwhelmed by just how different it is from everything I know. To me, Bangkok is so diverse and colorful. Beginning with the street-sellers, Tuk-Tuks, multicolors everywhere, it even has this unique exotic smell, and then there are the modern skyscrapers and a multitude of temples. Not to mention the mentality that's so different from ours."

"Now you just made me want to go there even more." My mom nudges my father's arm while smiling at Tasha. *Hint, hint, Dr. Grace.*

"I'm so glad for the opportunity of experiencing it as a local. It changes your entire perspective of a place when you get to explore it that way."

Scanning the room, I sigh in sheer contentment. *Oh, for goodness' sake, would you just stop?* I force myself to push down the lump forming in my throat back to the bottomless emotional pool it surfaced from. I leave my seat and take one next to Iris. "How are you doing?" I say.

Her kind smile climbs up to her eyes as she takes my hand in hers. "How are you feeling, precious? You lost some weight, didn't you?"

I study her pale, delicate face. She looks tired, light purple hue lining her eyes. Yet she looks much better than she had the last time I saw her. Maybe it's her inner joy that's reflecting from her eyes or her overall serene aura. "I'm doing well. You look better."

"There are days, and there are days." She squeezes my hand. "I'm going to get better. There's no chance I'll let anything prevent me from seeing my grandchild. Not even an asshole disease."

Tears pool at the corners of my eyes, and just before I'm about to embarrass myself in a hormones induced meltdown, my phone pings with a message. Reading the text, my eyes jump to Daniel's.

Daniel: Look at me, baby.

Sending me a soft smile, his thumbs work the screen.

Daniel: Ready to take a short break?

Sass pulls my lip up into a half-smile.

Ready to up my Daniel intake by a bazillion percent, ASAP!

Not more than five minutes later, Daniel locks the laundry room door behind us and turns to me.

I thread my finger through his belt loop, pulling him to me. I watch him, his eyes smiling at me. Tan and scruff enhance his handsome features, scars accentuated by the low-hanging lamp. "Looking very handsome tonight, Mr. Stark." Handsome is such an understatement for Daniel in gray slacks and a white button up.

"You look like something I can't take my eyes off of," he says to my neck. "Or can't wait to taste." His lips touch my skin. "Touch." His hand hovers over my breasts. I close my eyes with the surge of pleasure. "Bite." He lightly bites my earlobe. "Devour." His mouth seals on mine and does just that.

Chapter 32: After Midnight

I fluff the pillow, making sure that what I've properly concealed is hidden underneath. Waiting for Daniel to come out of the shower, I turn to give myself another look in the walk-in closet mirror. My lips tip up. Daniel will definitely be pleased with my attire. The blush-pink babydoll is demure and sexy at the same time. The underwire cups enhance everything that's already naturally enhanced while the silk garment ends just shy of my knee, spilling softly over my skin. To the sound of the bathroom door cracking open, I switch the light off and return to the bedroom.

"Oh hi," Daniel says, feasting his eyes on me. Sending his arm to my waist, he pulls me closer. Pressed against his freshly bathed chest, I take a lungful of heady Daniel scent. "Now, you look like the perfect dessert." I smile under the press of his lips on mine. Daniel's right hand on my waist tightens while his other trails over my bare back down to my silk-clad rear. When his lips touch my neck, tracing kisses down my shoulder, I squint my eyes to check the time.

"I think everyone really enjoyed themselves tonight." I stall for time, waiting for the clock to strike midnight.

"Yeah, especially your father." Daniel feathers his tongue over my collarbone.

I close my eyes, giving in to the sensation of Daniel's talented mouth on my skin. "He seemed to have warmed up to you by the second glass of scotch. Guess, we'll just have to keep him inebriated."

"Maybe we should stop talking about your dad when I'm seconds away from desecrating his precious daughter."

I squint at the clock. Easing off, I tip my head up at Daniel. "Um, before any desecration takes place, there's something I want to give you. Though hold that thought for later." I give him a suggesting smile, which he mirrors.

"You are all I ever need," Daniel says in a husky voice, his hand sliding into my panties.

Fondly, I push him back. He eyes me in humored surprise as I shake my head. I point my finger, gesturing for him to sit on the bed.

Daniel chuckles. "Bossy . . ." He drops himself back to the bed. Lying on his back with his head on his folded arms, he sends me his inviting askew smile.

I take a seat next to him under his persistent stare. "It's officially after midnight," I say and lean in to press a supple kiss on his lips. "Happy birthday." I deepen the kiss.

Daniel watches me with an easy smile as I ease to sit and send my hand to my pillow. I get the wrapped gift, which all of a sudden doesn't seem as awesome as I thought it would be. I hold it to my chest, worrying my lips for a stretched beat.

"Isn't this the part in which you're supposed to give me the gift?" Daniel asks, his lip tipped up.

I press the present tighter to my chest. "I don't know. It doesn't seem as great right now. Forget about it. Um, I'll get you something else."

Daniel inches to sit, holding his hand out. "It's mine, right?" I slightly lean backward, keeping his hand away. He shakes his head, and I find myself flat on my back, my hands pinned above me and the wrapped gift in Daniel's hand. "I'll release you only if you promise to behave." His eyes dance in joy, assessing me.

Seeing as I don't have many options, I reluctantly say, "Okay."

"Fine." He releases me but not before planting a noisy kiss on my lips. He arches a scarred brow in mocked warning.

I raise my hands, signaling I'm not going to break my promise. Covering my eyes with my hands next, I watch him unwrap my gift through my fingers. Focused, Daniel observes the vintage leather journal. I let my hands drop to my thighs, watching him attentively as he flips the cover and reads the dedication.

35 years of you has made this world a wonderful and better place. Happy Birthday. Love, H.

The look in Daniel's eyes as he gazes at me causes butterflies to flutter around my stomach, en masse.

"Um, before you go on," I say. "Maybe I had better explain what it actually is." A timid smile suffuses my lips. "These illustrations, the story they tell, hinge around me falling for you."

Holding the notebook in one hand, Daniel shifts to rest on the headboard. He motions for me to sit closer to him, and I do, settling myself between his parted legs, I ease back to lean on his chest.

With his hands around me, Daniel sets the notebook on my bent legs. Slowly he turns the page to the first sketch. A sketch of me looking down at a stain on my white blouse, frowning, captioned by "Is that a request?" A light chuckle comes from behind me, followed by a kiss on my hair and a turn of a page. My lips pull up to the next drawing of me wrapped in Daniel's embrace on a dancefloor. The sketch I've entitled *The Best Kiss of My Life*. It's a caption of the night I realized he was it for me. After a silent moment, Daniel brings his hand to my cheek, turning it for his mouth to meet mine for a kiss that doesn't fall short of the one portrayed in charcoal.

Securing his embrace around me, Daniel resumes turning the pages, each representing another snippet of the story of us. My heart flutters when he takes his time observing the sketch of him with a guitar cradled in his arms, next to a bonfire. "Hales." My name is a soft whisper.

"True," I say to the words decorating said sketch. The Night You Stole My Heart. The way he kisses me next, the tenderness, the slow, gentle touches that gradually develop into sensual seduction, make us pause for a few good moments that end with our breaths labored and tangled sheets.

In our own little bubble of us, we go through the pages. When Daniel turns the next one, our chuckle comes out in unison. It's a drawing of me, wrapped in a cardigan, a garter peeps from under the sweater, my expression of a deer caught in the headlights.

"This is gold. Probably one of my favorite times ever," Daniel says amused. He's referring to the time I surprised him at his office for a little sexy time rendezvous, dressed as a highly paid escort girl, only to find a room full of people staring at me as if I were indeed a member of the soliciting community. When our chuckles wind down, Daniel resumes turning the pages.

My heart squeezes a little when Daniel says, "Best decision of my life," to the illustration of a small square box nestled in an open glove compartment, also known as his proposal. The same pang returns to the sketch of Daniel walking on a seashore with a little single candle cupcake in his hand. What made my twenty-fourth birthday one of the most memorable ones. The next page, the one after the drawing of my hand with my engagement ring, makes him stiffen behind me. I slowly turn my head to look up at him.

"A girl?" he asks, his voice holding a beautiful candor of awe and emotions.

I swallow over the immediate lump in my throat, trading glances with Daniel's eyes and the drawing of a pregnancy test stick with the words "it's a girl" in the little window. Choked up, I nod. *These mushy, girly hormones are going to be the end of me.*

With utter tenderness, Daniel closes the notebook and sets it aside. With no less tenderness, he lays me back on the bed. Crawling on top of me, he holds himself above me. Soulful hazel eyes gaze at mine. Slowly, he leans in, his stare back and forth between mine and my parted lips till he is close enough for his mouth to brush mine. Soft kisses dot my face, my mouth, the corner of my lips, my eyes. "Thank you." The words travel from his mouth into mine. I close my eyes, savoring his taste. When his mouth leaves mine after long, intoxicating minutes, it's only to trail down, to relish every piece of my skin. As though unwrapping a delicate gift, he carefully slides the fabric of my negligee up my thighs, and higher, following the heaping garment with warm kisses. My eyes softly close as his tongue slowly traces a scorching path between my hipbones, just below my swollen belly. It feels like time stops as Daniel cherishes my body, gently and painstakingly affectionate.

Chapter 33: First Public Showing

Two months later

I'm taken aback by the sporadic flashes coming from the theatre's entrance hall. "Oh, there are photographers," I murmur. To say that Urban Heartbreak's premiere is extravagant would be stretching it, wildly. But apparently, modest as it is, it still drew in a few news outlets to cover the low-budget, indie film premiere.

To my sudden hesitation, Daniel, who's holding my hand, turns my way. "You okay?"

I tip my chin ahead. "Didn't take that into account."

Daniel searches my eyes. Reading my concern, he says, "I don't think they'll be interested in anyone but the cast."

"Besides one B-list actress, they're all unknown." I worry my lips. "I'm sure your presence here will make at least a tiny splash. *You'll* get noticed, that's for sure." My eyes drop to my belly. If they catch me on camera this time, it will look as though I had more than a burrito. Maybe three burritos with extra beans and a jug of Coke. The thought of making the tabloids again makes me stay put. To think they may somehow bring back the last time Daniel's name was mentioned and the reason, especially in my current condition, doesn't appeal, to say the least. "The reason your name was mentioned in the tabloids the last time is still sort of fresh. I don't want them somehow linking it to me being pregnant and . . . that."

Daniel nods, his jaw clutched firmly. "What do you want to do, then?"

I look up, meeting his stare. Weighing the options, I take his hand in mine again. "Let's just get in. Whatever happens, we'll just go with it." The last part comes out on an exhale.

"Mr. Stark, Mr. Stark!" *Immense surprise.* An insistent photographer tries to get Daniel's attention the moment we enter his periphery. Seeing there's really nothing we can do to prevent being photographed, I turn in my spot, my body flush against Daniel and press a kiss to his mouth hoping to take the attention from my bump to the lip lock. On the way, I make sure Daniel's body is blocking mine.

Tipping back a little to look at me, Daniel says in a low voice, only for me to hear. "Talk about just going with it."

As we make our way inside the venue, the photographer gives me a thumbs-up. I wink at him, making sure my large envelope clutch is concealing the part of me I rather not have captured on camera.

I look around, searching for Tasha, who should be getting here any moment now. Her flight landed about an hour ago. I'm excited to see her again and surprising Ian at the same time. It's been two months since I saw her last. Video chats have nothing on genuine bestie's face-to-face, heart to heart, quality time. I manage to give Ian a quick hug and whisper a few words of encouragement before he is swept away, again, for group photos or whatever movie people do on premier nights. The reception is a relatively intimate and elegant affair. Bubbly drinks served by a couple of all-black donning servers. The sounds of elated conversations, laughter, and some infrequent demands by the photographers blend with the pleasant instrumental music. When the lanky adorably flustered producer concludes his brief speech with a skittish toast, the guests drink up and join him and his cast in the theatre.

Darkness casts the room and the curtain slowly rolls up. I thread my fingers with Daniel's. I lean my head on his shoulder.

"Sorry. Um, ah, sorry," a familiar voice whispers. I straighten, watching Tasha wobble into the empty seat I saved beside me.

"You made it." I hug her tightly.

"Barely." Smoothing out the creases of her dress, she raises her eyes to the stirring in the row before us. Ian's radiant smile shines at her. They both rise a little to hug over Ian's seat.

I expect Ian to comment in Ian fashion about Tasha being late. No banter comes out of his lips, though. He seems to be rendered speechless. His sentimental look back and forth between the two of us tightens my chest. Biological or not, we're the only family supporting him here tonight.

As Ian turns back and the credits show on the screen, I tilt my head closer to Tasha's. "I called his mom," I whisper. Doubt laced concern fills her eyes. "I told her about the premiere and said her name will be on the guest list."

"What did she say?"

"She didn't hang up on me."

"Progress."

We both turn to the screen as the music in tandem to the title fades out and the first scene begins. I snuggle under Daniel's arm, watching the screen in utter awe and with an immeasurable sense of pride. Watching Ian bringing Dean, a tortured soul from the wrong side of the tracks, to life is mesmerizing. It's Ian up there on the screen, but nothing about that Ian is familiar. His traits, his stance, even his drawl is so rough and . . .

"Heaven help me, he's so . . . badass." Tasha completes my thoughts in a breathy, enthralled exclamation.

Halfway through the plot, my eyes mist over at the oh-so-expected tear-jerking "all is lost" moment. Or as I like to call it, "I want you so much but, love of mine, we can't be together. But no worries. The great forces to be are rooting for us, so bear with me for the next couple of scenes, okay?" I chance a glance to my right. As expected, Daniel appears to be painfully tortured. While to my left, Tasha is a sniffling, weepy mess.

George Washington once said, "To be prepared for war is one of the most effective means of preserving peace." *And prepared, I am.* Digging into my purse, I produce item number one from the survival kit. "D." I inch up to reach Daniel's ear. My disruption appears to be more than welcomed. I give him a thin smile, handing him a little flask. Taking the little silver bottle, he looks at me in question. I wink in place of an explanation, watching him open the bottle and take a quick drink. He sighs in relief, mouthing a humored, "Thank you" while rolling his eyes in an "I'm dying here" gesture. He throws back the rest of the drink.

Pursuing my humanitarian aid, I place a stack of balsam tissues on Tasha's lap. Transfixed by the events on the big screen, her eyes remain cemented to the action while she sends her hand to the tissues. She pats the paper under her eyes. Paper balled in her palm, Tasha rests her hand against her lips, watching Ian as Dean drive off toward the sunset on a black Harley.

With my work complete, I dig into my clutch once more, this time for a small pack of M&M's. *For the baby. Mother material, right there.* I bring a handful of candy to my mouth. I pivot my eyes sideway, sensing Daniel's stare on me. Under the dim glow coming from the screen, his smile caresses me. He gestures for me to lean closer. Shoving the chocolate into my mouth, I follow orders. Daniel sends his hand to the nape of my neck, pulling me into a deep kiss. Breaking the kiss, he eases back with a side grin and a couple of my M&Ms in his mouth. I glare at him, an action that only makes that sexy scarred lip climb higher.

Chapter 34: We All Have to Start Somewhere

"Hales." Tasha nudges me with her elbow. Unenthusiastically, I turn away from the offered platter of mini cakes and wine being served after the screening. I search for what she gestures at with tense green eyes. Unspoken, we find each other's hands for a hold. Silently, we watch Ian as he walks toward his mother, his demeanor a display of restraint and caution.

"I can't believe she came after all." The words leaving my mouth saturated with wonder.

We hold our breath, watching them talk. When the mother leans forward to give her son an uncertain embrace, our exhales come out as one. They exchange a few more words before she brushes the hair from his forehead and pats his cheek adoringly. She squeezes his hand and turns on her heels, scurrying out the building, as though terrified to miss curfew. Her vigilant behavior reinforces my assumption that her husband isn't aware of her whereabouts.

"So which one of you biatches called my mother?" Ian asks, snatching Tasha's drink from her hand and tossing it back daytime soap opera style.

Tasha tilts her head, squinting her eyes my way. Ian pins me with a lengthened gaze before wrapping me in his arms. He kisses my cheek. "Thank you."

I say nothing, hugging him back.

"Can I steal him from you, ladies?" Josh's question makes me take a step back.

Tasha and I wait for Ian as he says good-bye to Josh, who is flying out to visit with his family before starting his new job. Given Tasha is back for a day and Josh is leaving soon, it was unanimously decided that the three of us should make the most of the reunion and spend the night and the next day together till Tasha leaves.

Ian grabs Josh for a healthy cheerio kiss, and I look anywhere but at the steam-producing duo. When my eyes land on Tasha, I grimace. Just as she watched Ian on the screen less than an hour ago, she raptly observes him tonguing Josh's tonsils out.

"How about giving the young couple some privacy," I say, waving my hand before her eyes.

"That's," she blinks, "so hot."

My lips set in a fine line. "So, hi, that's our Ian, *not Dean*! Ogling our semi-brother making out with his boyfriend, who's my former boss, is wrong on so many levels." I tug on her arm. Finally, she breaks her gaping. "Lack of action in Thailand?" I ask. "Rafa not functioning too well in the humid climate?"

That sobers her up completely. "Let's not talk boyfriends for the next twenty-four hours, okay?" she says vehemently.

Questions jump to the tip of my tongue. I choose to swallow them back, what with the little scary, warning look she has on me.

. . .

"This room is so gorgeous. I want to lay you down on the floor and slow bone you as a token of my sincere gratification," Ian says, giving the room I got us for tonight another appreciative glance.

"The last time someone showed me his sincere gratification, I got knocked up, so I'll pass. Thank you, though." I finish my words with a curtsy.

Ian snorts while Tasha raids the minibar. Both Thing One and Thing Two seem more happy with the luxurious suite than I expected. I leave out the fact that Daniel was the one who actually got us the room for tonight, taking into account Tasha's request not to mention boyfriends tonight and Ian's beau being away on his special night. Boys suck. Except mine, that is. He is on a higher level of existence than the rest of the "boy" species.

"Okay, we're good to go!" Tasha says after ordering most of the items on the room service menu. Everything besides dishes with coriander. There's some long and dark history with Missy and the poor herb. Trying to get to the bottom of it is ill-fated. No man who ever tried lived to tell the tale, or at least, that's what she claims.

We dedicate the next fifteen minutes before the food to exploring the wealth the suite offers, which births the brilliant idea of dining in the hot tub. Like excited little kids, we scatter our separate ways to find something to wear that's hot tub appropriate. Meeting back in the great room, each wrapped in a snuggly white robe, we grin at one another like complete idiots.

I raise a warning finger at Ian. "I swear, if you're naked under that robe, I won't be held accountable for my behavior."

"What's hidden under this robe is too sacred to be shared with the likes of you," he says with such animation that Tash and I can't help but crack a smile.

A knock at the door has Tasha squeal and get her purse.

Snuggled in a thick robe, I sit on the edge of the tub with my legs in the warm water. Pregnancy and hot tubs don't go hand in hand. I look around and smile. Tasha in a tank top and panties, Ian in boxers, warm water up to their chests, mellowing out in the balcony's hot tub. An assortment of aromatic dishes covers the edge of the tub beside me while we talk and taste *everything*. The look Tasha and Ian exchange next doesn't escape me. It pokes as though they've just said something behind my back.

"Speaking of food," Tasha says, twisting her mouth.

Brace yourself, Hayley, here forth comes the kitty out of the bag.

"So what's the story with what's-her-face?" Ian scratches his chin, attempting to conjure up the name.

"What's the story with that Nadine person?" Tasha helps out.

"Pardon?" I say over a giggle.

"Oh, we're on to you." Ian narrows his eyes at me. "Hayley Jasmine Grace, before you're off feeding from other people's pots, may we remind you that blood is thicker than broth?"

"Did you really just say that?" I laugh it off.

"You cannot just flock with someone else when our feathers are still warm."

What does that even mean? I let out another rolling laugh. The solemnity Ian is trying to pull off has the opposite effect with the nonsense coming out of his mouth. I can't stop grinning. "Can you just stop with the moronic analogs; they don't make any sense. What's your angle, peaches?" I scoot over and plunge my legs in the water between Ian and Tasha.

"The two of you seemed quite cozy on Thanksgiving if you ask me." Tasha contributes her two cents.

"Anything we need to worry about?" Ian adds and Tasha nods. "We weren't born yesterday, gorgeous. We know full well that distance does make the heart grow adulterer-ier."

"It's amazing how all sense of commitment goes away when good food is involved," Tasha says drily.

I straighten up, looking at them both. "Okay, first off, there's no such thing as 'adulterer-ier,' and the correct saying, I believe, is distance makes the heart grow *fonder*." I shake my head with a smile. "And you two idiots are like the platonic loves of my life. So no matter how warm someone's oven is, or how alluring her cookie, no one could ever take your place." I grin. "But she's pretty cool, right?"

They both shrug and murmur, "Yeah, so what."

"Okay now, let's move on to an awesome movie premier." I smile at Ian. In a once-in-a-lifetime occasion, Ian appears coy.

"I loved the movie so much I want to marry it and have its beautiful children," Tasha gushes, her eyes dreamingly twinkling at Ian.

Ian radiates a smile that increases the stars in her eyes. "What did *you* think about it, Hales?" There's not a trace of cheer in the question. He studies me sternly, waiting for me to give him what I believe is an honest response.

"I think it had a solid plot, and your acting was perfect, really. C'mon, Tash here has a mini crush on Dean."

Ian's lip twitches, but just a little.

"I'm not the ultimate chick-flick fan, but still, it held my interest and even made me shed a tear . . . or two when Dean drove off, leaving Blythe heartbroken."

Ian nods, disappearing for a short pensive beat. He shrugs, his expression grim. "We all have to start somewhere, right?"

The frown on Tasha's and my face must be identical. "What are you saying?" Tasha utters our unified thoughts.

"I've been given this amazing chance, and I couldn't be more grateful. But I've been thinking, and this is not what I want to do.

I'd rather work on projects that mean something, and I know that to make it happen I need to be better. This was a fluke, which I'm still having a hard time wrapping my head around. How in the hell did I get this opportunity." He shakes his head with a hint of a dismayed smile. "I'm going to take acting classes. That's what I'm going to do next. Well, at least before attempting auditioning again."

I squeeze his shoulder. "Good for you."

"That's great." Tasha kisses Ian's cheek.

I look down at an appetizer in my hand. "So I have some news as well," I begin. "I signed with an agent. Apparently, she really likes my illustrations and already has this project in mind for me that sounds interesting." My friends are kissing me this time.

Tasha's expression turns sentimental. "I'm having a great time in Thailand and love what I'm doing. But I miss home and you guys so much."

They rise to stand and the three of us huddle in a tight embrace, our foreheads touching.

"You know that's exactly how a good porn starts . . . a blonde, a brunette, and a stud getting it on in a hot tub," Ian manages to say before we both dunk him into the water and keep him under for a few long, sweet seconds.

. . .

"Hales?" Daniel says as he spots me at his home office door. His stare drops to his watch and back at me. "Everything okay?"

I take silent steps till I reach him. Reading my intentions, he rolls his chair back to allow me enough space to nestle in his lap. He covers me in a warm, most anticipated embrace, prompting a little sigh from my mouth. I look up. "I missed you."

His eyes crinkle so sweetly. "What about your friends?" He

presses a soft kiss to my forehead.

"They passed out right after the hot tub and a couple of bubbly bottles. And before you ask, I had soda." His smile grows. I inch up a little for my lips to touch his bristled jaw. "I'll go back before they wake up tomorrow morning. I just wanted . . . this."

His hug around me tightens. I burrow my face in his t-shirt clad chest. Indulging in the feel of the soft fabric and perfect, warm Daniel scent. He lets me snuggle for a while, his nose and lips nuzzling in my hair in turns. When I yawn, he tips my head up with his finger. "Take you to bed?"

I shake my head. "It's pretty amazing right here." He kisses my lips and lets me cocoon right back. Holding me with one arm, he types with the other, allowing me to soak in him as he works.

I'm not sure how much time has passed till I feel him carry me to our bed. When he covers us and wraps his arms around me, I fall asleep even deeper with a smile on my lips.

Chapter 35: A Synonym for Perfection

Three months later

I fight my droopy eyelids to open. Blinking a couple of times, the unfamiliar blurry surrounding comes into view. Colors and shapes blend, revealing a washed, formless scene. A voice softly says my name through the blur. It's familiar and soothing. *Daniel*? my mind says, but my lips, heavy and dry, are unable to cooperate. My voice stays inside of me. *Daniel?* I try again. Nothing comes out. I hear voices around me while I'm floating above, struggling to keep my eyes open. When a warm hand is placed on my cheek, I drift into nothingness once again.

When I finally manage to force my eyes open, the room has dimmed. A soft beam of light comes from beside me in the otherwise murky room. I try to swallow over the aridity in my mouth, letting out a small cough instead. Still drowsy, I look around, taking in the natural tones of what appears to be an ample suite.

"You're up," Daniel's voice whispers from somewhere near. My mind is in such a muddle that I failed to notice him sitting closely to the other side of the wide bed.

For a confusing moment, I stare at him as he softly smiles at me in a dark Henley, holding a light pink bundle in his arms. My eyes trail from his beaming ones to the pink bundle and back, and it hits me, hard. Everything comes back to me, flashing before my eyes like scenes from a fast-paced action movie. Arriving at the hospital, the persistent pain in my lower back, the delivery room, conversations in low voices, hazel eyes full of concern and anxiety, being rushed in a gurney, right until the mask that covered my mouth and nose, to the quiet darkness that came right after.

His free hand finds mine. "You want to see her?"

I nod, anxious. Gently, as though she's too fragile to hold, he tilts her upwards, revealing the rosy little face to me.

There are moments in life that just catch you off-guard, no matter how long you've prepared for them. Moments that no matter how much thought you've given them, or the anticipation that has built inside of you, you're still not ready for. For nine months, you carry a little human inside of you, talk to it, feel it move, kick, bond with it, dream about it. But nothing, *nothing,* can prepare you for the instant you actually meet your child. I look at her, and with one sole awed glimpse, my heart multiplies to accommodate all the love I never thought was even possible. My eyes trail from my baby to Daniel, and that's all it takes to bring all the emotions I'm feeling into something so painfully sweet and overwhelming. The look he has on our little girl makes me fall in love with him all over again.

"You want to hold her?"

Still rendered speechless by my outgrowing emotions and awe, I nod. Unable to take my eyes from them both, I watch Daniel rise to stand and settle on the bed beside me. Carefully, he places our daughter in my arms. I study the little baby sleeping on me and swallow over the lump of immense bliss in my throat. Daniel brings a glass of water from the nightstand and places the straw in my mouth. When I'm done, he sets the glass back and wraps his arm around my shoulders.

"She's so tiny and beautiful," I whisper.

"That, she is."

I look up at him, mesmerized yet again by the look in his eyes, on her, on me. "Kiss me," I say in a soft voice. And he does. Kissing me gently and slowly, conveying with his kiss the magnitude of the moment.

"What are we going to name her?" I ask as we ease back.

He shakes his head in thought. "What's the synonym for perfection?"

You.

We smile at each other. Daniel kisses me before sitting up. "Hungry?"

"Famished."

His lopsided smile makes an appearance. "Why don't I give my girls some alone time and go get food?"

My girls . . . I smile back at him, watching him as he crouches to press a gentle kiss on the fair down on our daughter's head. Tilting his head to catch my eyes, his lip tips up before we meet for a chaste kiss. My eyes remain on him till he leaves the maternity suite.

"Hi you," I whisper to the sleeping wonder in my arms. My eyes caress over her delicate features, her pinkish heart-shaped lips, the delicate fluttering eyelids. She is right here in my arms and it's still hard to comprehend that I'm actually holding my daughter, our daughter.

When Daniel enters the room more than twenty minutes later, my heart does a little somersault. This time, it's not as a gesture of appreciation to everything that he is, but to what he carries in his hands. *Bless you, D. Bless you.*

It's been over two hundred and forty days since sushi and I parted ways. It felt almost morbid saying good-bye and all the more painful keeping my distance. The next few good moments are dedicated to our reunion. At first, I'm a bit hesitant, fumbling with the long sticks, finding the right angle to take the precious bundles into my mouth. Gradually my confidence grows and they slide into me, one after the other.

"I'm getting jealous over here." Daniel gives me a wicked look from across the room, where he cuddles our little baby, lulling her to sleep in a rocking chair.

Inwardly beaming, I send my tongue out to lick the soy sauce from around the roll's thin dark warp. Taking the chubby piece into my mouth, I close my eyes and moan. Opening my eyes, I smile at Daniel, who watches my little show with a sinister smile.

I shake my head, my lips mirroring his. "Way too early, dude . . . Didn't you hear the doctor? Six weeks!"

Wicked grin intact, he says, "I see your mouth is in pristine condition, though. Fancy that."

Our humored glances lock, and we break into a light unified chuckle. A healthy wail bursts the moment. *How can something so delicate and sweet produce such a deafening noise?*

. . .

We lie in silence, facing each other, our cheeks resting on plump pillows. Daniel traces the smattering of freckles on my nose with the pad of his finger. His finger slowly descends to my lips. I give it a supple kiss before it continues to my jaw.

"It feels surreal," I say in a thin voice, not to wake the fed, deeply sleeping baby in the crib next to the bed. "She's so precious."

We exchange a gratified stare. His features turn somber. "You scared me earlier." His hand cups my cheek, his thumb caressing my skin. "I was actually terrified when they said the two of you were in danger. It made me realize that up until that moment, there was one person I'd always put above myself. Now, there are two."

I bring my hand to cover his that's on my cheek.

"Remember when you asked me how I felt about moving to Baja for a while?"

"Yes." I search his eyes, somewhat confused by the sudden question.

"Do you still want to do that?"

"Can *you* really do it?"

He nods, contemplating. "I'd have to prepare. It can't happen immediately. I thought, maybe in a couple of months. You can work on that project of yours and Iris can help with the baby now that she's getting stronger. I think it'll do her good, having us close to her."

"I think it will do all of us good. I think it's perfect."

Chapter 36: Moment in Time

Daniel

Six months later

Surfboard under one arm and baby huddled under the other – a flailing and gurgling bundle of contagious, angelic giggles – I head toward the water. I straddle the board, holding Emma in my arms so she's facing me, and let the waters slowly rock us in calming little sways. She looks at me with those big brown eyes, full of joy, making my chest double with adoration and pride.

She brings her little hands to tap the board's surface, splashing water on us. Her eyes grow bigger with ecstasy along with her smile.

"Hey Em, say daddy. Da-ddy." She lets out a string of sweet blabber that makes my lips stretch so wide. Taking in her amazing resemblance to Hayley, I smile at her. With the thought of her resemblance to her mom and how she'd probably look when she's older, I try another word.

"Repeat after Daddy, Em. Celibacy." She giggles. "Say it, Em. Ce-li-ba-cy." The sweet rolling sound continues with more water splashing. I chuckle and mutter, "No joking now. It's a serious matter." I take her in my arms, hugging her close to my chest and inhaling her powdery scent. I sit her with her back to me, embracing her with one arm while paddling gently with the other. For a while, we float on the board, just me and my baby girl, enjoying the peacefulness till it's time to get ready.

. . .

"She looks like a little angel, doesn't she? Aren't you, tiny one?" Julie, Hayley's mom, kisses Emma's bouncy curls. Emma looks up at me with her smiley, gleaming eyes, holding her arms out. When I take her in mine, she rewards me with a sweet, happy sound.

"She's a mini Hayley, eh?" I plant a kiss on Emma's tiny nose. Stretching my arms up, I hold her above me, making her smile brighter.

"She is. It's like seeing Hayley as a baby all over again," Julie confirms, smiling at us both. "Though, I think that smile of hers is you."

I grin at Emma, studying her slightly crooked, adorable smile. "You got Daddy's smile? Sorry for that, Em."

Julie squeezes my bicep, shaking her head humoredly. "We should get going. Do you want me to hold Emma?"

I shake my head. "We want her to be a part of it."

Julie's eyes mist over. "I better go now. Congratulations, darling." She gives me a one-arm hug before stepping out the patio door and heading toward the beach.

"Let's makes this happen, Em. You ready?"

Everyone is waiting on the white sand of our Baja home slice of private beach. Under the soft afternoon sun and light, warm breeze, Ian and Josh, Natasha and Rafa, Iris, looking healthier with eyes shining and some ruddiness on her cheeks, Steven, Hales' brother, his mother by his side and right next to her the only person who doesn't smile at me. There's a hint of warmness in Dr. Grace's otherwise solemn stare. That sliver of affection goes to the baby. *I bet my left nut on it.*

"Thanks to you, baby girl, we finally made it here," I whisper to Emma. She titters when I say, "Your mother finally agreed to get married when you were born, so Em, I owe you big time." Emma looks at me with shiny eyes and lets out a string of adorable noises.

Noticing everyone's attention gradually shifting toward the house, I turn my gaze. With a shy smile caused by the attention, Hayley walks toward us in a simple white dress and small white flowers in her hair. However, nothing about her is simple. The light wind sways loose curls away from her delicate, freckled face, the soft sun bringing out her exquisite beauty. I'm sure the wild pummeling of my heart is bruising my ribcage.

I drink her in.

It's the breath you're holding because she's still a step away. It's this feeling you feel that's somewhere between bliss and pain. Another step, and another, her eyes meet mine and she smiles a smile that trickles into me. A flinch of ache constricts my chest with that smile because it's in response to me. I take her hand in mine and walk the three of us together. Reaching the priest, Hayley bites on a mischievous smile, winking at me. Unspoken, she sends me a private message I read loud and clear. It's somewhere along the lines of here I am, *yours*, forever and for always.

I grin at her, closing the gap between us. When I lean in to chastely kiss her cheek, she shifts her head so our lips meet. As our mouths touch, there's nothing chaste about it anymore.

"There's a wedding night for that, gorgeous," Ian says, his words followed by a wave of short laughter around us.

The priest clears his voice, humor coloring his eyes as he looks at us. "You're about to make promises to each other." He starts then Emma cuts him off with some demanding noises, asking to be held by her mom. Hayley takes her from me. Our baby looks at Hayley for a sweet moment and then makes it clear she wants to go back to me. Crowing and gurgling, wriggling my way with the most beautiful smile.

"Can't really blame her," Hayley says with a smile of her own and shrugs. A few chuckles surround us as I take Emma back into my arms.

"Amen to that," Ian says. I shake my head and nod at the priest to carry on.

"Here, you'll vow to be there for one another, take care of each other, find happiness and bliss together." The intimate ceremony resumes, with these words, our closest people, the sounds of waves, and delightful baby tittering. As I slide the ring on Hale's finger, I tip down to whisper in her ear, "No going back, Mrs. Stark."

Slowly, she lifts her eyes to mine, her lips stretching into a gentle smile. She puts the ring on my finger, pulling on my hand to slightly make me bend till my ear is close to her lips. "You're stuck with me now, Husband." We hold a beaming stare.

"You may kiss the bride."

"This will require my complete attention," I say, winking at Hales. I turn to look at the people behind us and hand Emma to Ian. "Start practicing, man."

"Hey," I say to Hayley before lifting her in my arms. I let her slide just enough for our mouths to meet. Subtly touching my lips to hers, I gaze into her eyes. Like in a slow dance, our mouths part. Unhurriedly closing the distance. Slowly meshing with one another. Hayley's eyes flutter closed, mine follow as I savor her taste, her nearness. I hold her close to me, our mouths fusing in a perfect, sensual match. We slowly ease back, smiling at each other, bonded in a union that's sacred beyond words. Hayley's heavy leaded stare as though she's drunk by my presence alone, makes me feel larger than life. No one in this universe could ever rise up to her level. No one out of an entire humanity is her.

When we take a step back and turn to face our family and friends, my smile turns into a smirk I'm trying hard to subordinate. Dr. Grace's glare on me can easily constitute as aggravated assault.

Congratulations and hugs fill in the next long moments. I let Hayley be the focus of that and step back to thank the priest and exchange a few civil words with my father-in-law.

Walking up to the house, my gaze follows Hayley as she's holding Emma with one hand, chatting with her friends and Iris. I look at her with fresh eyes. This incredibly striking woman. She's smiling her heart-stopping smile. A smile that shines from those big browns eyes. This woman in the flowy white dress over golden skin and loose waves. The mother of my daughter, my best friend, and the undeniable love of my life. My wife.

"Hey." Hayley tugs on my hand as we step up the deck.

"Yes, Mrs. Stark?" I say with a grin.

"Um, when's the wedding night starting?"

My grin doubles. "On it. Let me just get rid of everyone."

Chapter 37: Breathe a Little Better

"Whatever our souls are made of, his and mine
are the same." –Emily Brontë

Four months later

I drop to a chair, my shoulders sagging as I observe the flotsam and jetsam of the day. Scream, run away, or at the very least, flip off the clatter around me – that's all I want to do. Clearly, it's not what I'll end up doing. *This being an adult thing sucks.*

Rolling my cotton dress' sleeves up, I mentally prepare myself to literally get my hands dirty. It's been one of those days when nothing gets done. An orgy of incomplete tasks. The kitchen counter full of dishes and baby bottles, boxes all around me labeled "Kitchen" in black sharpie. A mess that can only be described as white noise that is getting on my very last nerve. I push out a surrendered exhale and dig my hands in the sink. *Why don't you ever listen, ah?* Why do I always have to prove a point? Why couldn't I just say yay to hiring people for the unpacking part too? "Oh, c'mon, it's just a few boxes," I said. "I don't like strangers touching my stuff," I said. Not my finest stubborn hour.

I trip over a basket full of dirty clothes as I scramble to find a dishtowel to dry my hands. That's it. I'm calling someone first thing tomorrow morning.

Empowered by my decision, I reach for a bottled water. Something to do with the hand-mouth coordination miserably fails and a stream of cold water runs down the valley of my breasts. Observing the damage with irritation, reaching for the dishtowel again, I murmur, "Fuck me," under my breath.

A low chuckle comes from behind me. "Is that a request?"

I turn to see Daniel standing at the door, the very picture of hot, tall, and deliciously sinful. His scarred lip tipped, making my own lips follow suit. His crooked smile draws me in, and for a span of a moment, I'm lost in him.

His eyes roam over me, lazily stripping off my dress. I lick my lips, scanning him appreciatively from head to enticingly bare feet. "Oh, yeah," I say in a smoky voice. "It was indeed a request."

An extent of a blink is the exact length of time we manage to hold our faces straight. Our eyes, wrinkled at the corners, dance at each other. His light chuckle and my easy giggle meet. Daniel holds out his hand with a tilt of his head and a thin smile asking me to join him. I take a few steps to reach him, lacing my fingers with his.

In pleasant silence, we cross the inky lit living room. As though reading my thoughts, Daniel stops by Emma's room. Standing in the doorframe, we both pause to watch our Em, a sweet, serene expression on her adorable face. I rest my head on Daniel's shoulder, drawn to his warmth. And everything feels better. He dips to leave a kiss on my hair and tugs on my hand, signaling for me to follow him.

"What's that?" I say in surprise as we round the corner to the master bedroom of our Baja home. Nearly six months after tying the knot in this exact location, we finally moved in. From the door, I study the medium size, light blue box in the middle of our bed with two forks on its side.

Daniel pivots my way, his joyful eyes on me. "Brought you something from home."

I release my hold on him and near the bed. I lean in with two hands on the bed, my leg slightly raised up for balance, and read the label on the box. A wide grin colors my face in happiness. I turn my head to look at Daniel over my shoulder. "If I weren't already married to you, I would marry you all over again."

Daniel's bad-boy grin makes an appearance. "Just stay in this position with your sublime ass up in the air and we're good."

Biting on my smile, I slightly shake the praised body part. Before my next exhale, large hands grab me by my hips, pulling my ass back against his jean-clad groin. I let out a surprised squeal, finding myself unceremoniously flipped over on my back. Daniel nudges my legs apart, causing my knee-length dress to pile up in a heap of fabric on my hips. He holds himself above me by his arms on either side of my head, his face tipped down at me. A few clusters of golden hair fall on his forehead, nearly hiding his arched brow. "What will it be?" he says in husky timbre. "Me or the chocolate cakes in that box?"

I put on a grave expression, bringing my finger to my lips. I tap them lightly, twisting my mouth from side to side. I sigh. "Tough choice, to be honest." Daniel narrows his eyes at me, a ghost of a smile playing on his lips. "And just so you know, calling those Pavés 'chocolate cakes' is blasphemy!"

Daniel hangs his head down in defeat. He slightly shakes it from side to side, pushes himself to drop on his back beside me. "I never stood a chance, did I?"

I turn to lie on my side, facing him. "How about we share?" I wiggle my brows.

He cranes his neck to look at me, rolling his eyes animatedly.

"A moment, please." I smile. "I'm just going to change into something less wet." I wave at the front of my dress.

He shakes his head, stopping me by a grip on my wrist. "Just take it off." The rough edge of his voice seeps into my core, spreading warmth.

I lift my dress up my thighs and stop. "I'll show you mine if you show me yours."

A flirty grin adorns Daniel face as he sends his hand to the back of his shirt and pulls it over his head.

Sitting on the bed cross-legged in our underwear, facing each other, I ever so carefully lift the lid. "Beautiful," I say reverentially.

"Hales, it's a fucking cake."

I lightly shake my head, putting a finger to my lips, and shush him. I dip a fork in the layered delight of chocolate heaven and bring it to Daniel's mouth. His amused mouth closes around the fork. Retrieving the fork, I bring it to my own mouth, sucking on the taste of faint sweetness and Daniel. "Perfect," I murmur.

Taking a forkful for myself, I lick my lips and say, "Thank you for bringing me this cake all the way from home, I'm grateful for everything you do for me."

A soft smile comes as a response. "I'm grateful for everything you are."

I bring another spoonful to his mouth and lean in to press a kiss on his lips. He sends his hand to my cheek, in a soft caress trailing it down my neck. His finger moves along my bra strap, slowly reaching the mound of my breast. A light shiver runs through me as the palm of his hand hovers over the cup of my bra. His voice is a tone rougher as he says, "I'm grateful that even after all this time, this is your response to my touch."

My mouth dries and my lips part as he sets the box aside and pulls me to sit astride him. Daniel's lips trace the path of my skin his hand left a moment ago. His hands come to my waist, gently caressing up my back till they clutch around my shoulders. Gently, by the hold of his hand on my shoulders, he arches me back. His mouth descends to my bellybutton. In scorching kisses and a mix of gentle sucks and bites, he makes his way up my stomach, between my breasts, along my stretched neck. With one hand still holding me arched, his other splays between my breasts, slowly moving to lightly squeeze one while his mouth kisses the other. Through the lacy fabric, he sucks on my hardened nipple. A needy whimper floats from my lips. He eases back to push the fabric down, exposing my breast to him. He slowly bites on my nipple, only to soothe it with his tongue right after. The sensation spreads in my body in a warm wave. My breath becomes heavier when his free hand slides inside my panties. When I say his name on a breathy expel, he tilts me forward to look at him. With his eyes captivating mine, his fingers find me, and slowly, excruciatingly slow, dip into me. I hold his stare as I send my hand to his boxers, to wrap around him, high on the raw sound reverberating from his chest.

My hand sliding around him and his fingers working my desire, we meet for a wild kiss. Fighting for domination, for more. Consuming each other's taste with our mouths. Daniel lifts us up enough to free himself from his boxers, never breaking our kiss. A moan travels from my mouth to his when he pushes my panties aside and sinks into me. Moving around him, I cup his cheeks, my eyes swallowing him in. His brows set in concentration, his scarred lip agape, letting his labored breaths caress my lips. I tip enough for my tongue to roam over his lips, for my mouth to kiss the scar on his sharp cheekbone. The feel of him in me, the erotic sounds coming out of his lips as he pleasures me sends a surge of heat climbing up my thighs, washing over me in inconceivable pleasure. I'm quaking around him, my core shaken, a light shiver bathing me as I drop my head back and through moans of ecstasy say his name.

His hands swing to my waist, shifting my body so he can reach deeper in me. His grip on me becomes tighter as he works my body to ride him faster. When I tighten around him and call out his name this time, my name comes out of his lips in a strained harmony to his last forceful drives.

"I love you," I whisper next, rested on his chest, in his arms.

"Love you, Hales," Daniel says, tracing little circles on my skin.

It's just another day. Uneventful. Another day that when the first stars appear in the calm Baja sky; I linger for a brief moment on the patio, soaking in the exotic breeze that has become familiar, then return inside to our home, feeling utterly content and blissful. Utterly complete.

With our baby tucked in bed and me being held in the arms of my Daniel, I feel like I am filled to brimming and I breathe a contented sigh.

We both freeze at the demanding wail coming from the room next door.

"For fuck's sake," comes a husky grumble. "How can something so sweet reach those decibels?"

I lightly chuckle and murmur through a yawn, "Your turn."

I wait for a few moments to pass and for silence to blanket our home before tiptoeing to Emma's room. This never gets old. The sight of Daniel singing to our daughter, rocking her to sleep.

Yes, it's just another day. And it's everything I've ever wanted. And more.

From the Author

Thank you *so much* for taking the time to read OUTER CORE. If you enjoyed it, please consider leaving a review or recommending it to a friend. Thank you for your support!

Also, I more than love hearing from my readers, honestly, it's the best part of the whole writing process. So, send me an email at: author.sehrlich@gmail.com or chat with me on Facebook.

Thank you for allowing me to share my stories with you, and I hope to be re-invited to your bookshelf with my next releases.

Sigal

Acknowledgments

THANK YOU to every single person out there who read the series! Thank you for reviewing, messaging, emailing, loving, liking, and spreading the word.

* Just between you and me, I'm playing with the idea of a spin-off book about Ian and Tash. So maybe this isn't really the end of the Stark series period. . .

Big thank yous for those who helped, encouraged, and shared with me the fun experience of writing this book. Kiki, the most enormous thank you goes to you! Thank you for always willing to listen to my crazy stuff.

Sam, I'm incredibly grateful for your friendship and everything you are.

Nicole Hornbaker Langston, first and foremost, for getting me! For your great play with words, and making my writing beautiful. Reading your notes is almost as enjoyable as writing my stories.

Jenny, for always giving my work the last needed polish and perfect tweaks.

An excerpt from

Leaving Me Behind

An inner debate starts between my head and the rest of my instigated body. Wake him up and beg for more vs. control myself. The verdict rendered is based on the logic of probably never having this opportunity ever again. Enjoy it while it lasts. In other words: have that candy, life's too short.

Shutting the mental door on my manners, suppressing desires, mature behavior, and oh, self-respect, I slowly inch toward the bed. Contemplating how to approach the waking process, I decide to, ahem, return a favor, as they say. Slowly, I sit on the bed next to his handsome, serene self and reach ever so gently to remove the towel hugging his loins, allowing myself better access to wake him *up*. Having a fist full of the towel in my grip, with my head tilted toward my target, I hear a soft, embarrassingly petrifying chuckle. I'm not sure what occurs first, the eruption of flames that cover my face or the jump my eyes take to meet a very sexy, amused gaze. I must look like the girl caught with her hand about to violate the cookie jar. *Oh Lord, the road to ultimate self-humiliation never ends.*

The grin he sends me next, after I timidly smile at him, might have just disintegrated the stiches of my skimpy panties. His eyes turn to bore on me in tandem to his tongue playing with the edge of his front teeth. My heart starts to beat in double pace as the notion of what's coming next registers. My lips gape and the center of my body burns as, with my eyes still glued to his, I slowly lean in toward him. Abruptly, he breaks our promising eyes connection to look out the window.

"Mierda!" He jolts to sit. "Shit, shit." He jumps from the bed, his towel dropping to the floor, leaving him all bare and glorious before me. I try not to, but end up staring, of course. Who can really blame me? Some things were artfully crafted to be stared at.

"I'm going to miss my flight," he murmurs, his fingers push through his hair as he looks around the room on edge. "Where are my clothes?" He finally addresses me, bringing me back from my momentary fixation on him. I shake my stalking off.

"Um, just a sec," I say and head to get his clothes that are hung on the ropes on the back balcony. Not a second passes from the time he snatches the semi-wet pile from my hands till he starts shrugging them on, ridiculously hurried. Between buttoning his fly and shrugging on his shirt while almost losing his balance, he sends his thick metal watch a peep that results in a string of impressive swear words in Spanish. Something clicks in my head and I take a step back, fold my arms, and watch him. I have an urge to start clapping for the performance he is giving me. Best. Flitting-a-one-night-stand-excuse. Ever. The guy should quit his day job and pursue an acting career.

Buckling his belt, he finally lifts his mesmerizing dark eyes to acknowledge me. He takes a wide step to reach me, and before I realize what's going on, his hand cups the back of my neck and pulls me into one hell of a kiss. I gasp, and his mouth presses harder. I get sunk into the kiss until his lips gently release me, his hand still holding my neck. His breath mixes with mine as he says,

"I'll be traveling on business for the next three days. I want to see you when I get back." Another kiss and I watch the door as it closes after him.

Wow, *he is good. He is really good.* Not only has he managed to sneak away with no awkward, "Good-bye, hope to never see you again," but he actually made it somehow look promising. Not to me, anyway – maybe it would have worked on some pathetic airhead. *It's not going to happen.* He didn't even bother to ask for my number. I roll my eyes; a smile laced with scorn forms on my lips as I head to rip the sheets he slept on off my bed and throw them in the washing machine. I can't even cross this one off my bucket list because I couldn't have even allowed myself to imagine what he just did to me in the shower or even to imagine just . . . *him.* Even if I tried hard, really hard . . . still a solid no.

And what the hell is a delivery boy doing going on a business trip anyway. God, what a player. But who really cares. I've started experiencing the goods this new country has to offer, which, after all, was the crux of my grand plan.

Available now!

Also by Sigal Ehrlich

Retrace
Leaving Me Behind
Unplugged, coming spring 2016

About the Author

By teen age, Sigal already lived in three different continents where she was lucky enough to experience and visit varied places, meet unique people, which only helped fuel her overly developed imagination. Currently, Sigal calls Estonia home where she lives with her husband and three kids.

Not exactly sure where they will end up next …

Sigal would love to hear from you, please visit her on her website, Twitter, and Facebook.

http://www.sigalehrlich.com/
@Sigal_Ehrlich
https://www.facebook.com/sigalehrlich.author
http://www.pinterest.com/authorsehrlich/
auhtor.sehrlich@gmail.com